BELLA AND THE HAPPILY EVER AFTER

A LOVE ON THE TRACK NOVEL

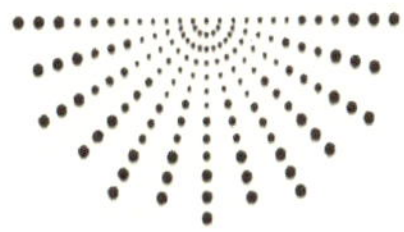

AMY SPARLING

BELLA

*V*alentine's Day is a little bit weird when you're not quite single but not quite in a relationship. I'm standing in the grocery store aisle that's been taken over with all things sugary, pink, and red. I was just swinging by here after my classes today to pick up a frozen pizza for dinner, but then this shiny aisle filled with last-minute shoppers caught my attention.

I could get Liam a card, but I don't know when I'll see him. His last race was a week ago and he's been in California filming interviews and talking about how he's leaving Team Loco for good. The fans are mad that he's leaving and press wants answers. He's supposed to be back home this week, where he'll move into his mom's house here in Roca Springs, but I don't know when that will be because last night he didn't have his flight scheduled yet.

Giving him a Valentine's Day card after Valentine's Day would be weird. Plus, I'd feel really awkward trying to find a card with a message that accurately describes how I feel about him.

I'm pretty sure they don't make Valentine's cards that say:

To the guy I've had a massive crush on for eight months, who used to make out with me but then went off to work as a professional athlete and now he's coming back and we'll get to be together but we're not quite together yet: Happy Valentine's Day

Hallmark should really get on that.

Moving past the greeting cards, I look at the array of Valentine's candy and stuffed bears and plastic crap that no one really needs. This holiday is kind of stupid if you ask me. Candy is good every day of the year. Why do you need an obligation to buy gifts for your loved one today?

I decide against getting Liam anything. After all, it's not like I'll see him today since he's still in California, and it's not like we're officially "lovers" yet. He told me last Thanksgiving that when he's off Team Loco for good he would ask me to be his girl-friend. That hasn't happened yet.

We've stayed in contact, talking every single day, but we're still not *official*-official. In my mind, he's my boyfriend, but in real life, we haven't put that label on it. My best friend Kylie knows all about this romantic arrangement, but I haven't told my mom. I especially haven't told my brother Brent, who kind of hates Liam as much as you can hate someone. I'm not sure what we're going to do about that, but I'm not about to give up on this relationship before we've even had a chance to start it.

Now that I'm in an awkwardly sad mood from thinking about Valentine's Day and my brother and Liam, I grab a frozen thin crust cheese pizza and head to the self-checkout lane. The sooner I can get home and eat my feelings, the better. Maybe next year I'll do something cheesy for Valentine's day with Liam, but not this year. This year, I'm still technically single. And single girls don't do anything for Valentine's Day.

THURSDAYS ARE RELAXING DAYS. I ONLY HAVE ONE college class in the morning this semester and then I get to go home and chill out for a while. Mom works until six every weekday, and Brent is away at Texas A&M. I might join him at his fancy university after I get my associate degree here at the local community college in town. Maybe I won't. I still have absolutely no idea what I want to do with my life. And if I'm going to spend tons of money in the form of student loans at a university, I need to know what I'm going to do with my life first.

But until that day comes, all I'm really doing with

my life is attending classes three days a week and then hanging out at home the rest of the time. Kylie's also attending college, but she's at the university an hour away, studying to become a teacher. Her family couldn't afford dorm life and she didn't want to go into too much debt with loans, so she's making the two-hour commute twice a week, on Tuesdays and Thursdays. I never see her on those days because she's too exhausted to hang out.

I try not to think about how it kind of sucks that I'm stuck home alone on Valentine's Day with a frozen cheese pizza. It's really not a big deal, I tell myself. Not at all.

Netflix is my friend today. I'm lounging on the couch in true epic slovenly fashion, halfway through a marathon of this home-buying reality show, when my doorbell rings. I startle from the unexpected noise, and then I hear the sound of a truck driving away from my house. Must be a package delivery for my mom.

When I open the door, it's not exactly a package sitting on my welcome mat. It's a large bouquet of flowers. Red and pink and white roses to be exact. My teeth dig into my bottom lip as I bend down and pick up the heavy glass vase. As far as I know, my mom isn't dating anyone, so that *should* mean that these are for me. My heart swells as I hobble into the kitchen with these heavy flowers and set them on the table. I really, really, hope they're for me.

I look around for the card that's hidden in the array of gorgeous roses, and finally find it. My name is on the outside of the little envelope and I exhale a sigh of relief. It's not like I was expecting anything, but now that my hopes are up, I really wanted these to be for me and not some accidental wrong delivery.

I open the envelope and pull out the card, expecting to see Liam's name on it.

Your real present is outside.

I frown. What does that mean? I didn't see any other packages out there…

Opening the front door, I look down at the welcome mat. Nothing. Maybe I mis-read the card. Or—

Liam walks up from the side of my porch, wearing black jeans, a blue button up shirt, and that signature smirk of his.

"Surprise," he says, holding out his arms to me. I walk straight into them, crushing him in a hug. I am enveloped by the intoxicating scent of his cologne, and the warm, perfect feeling of his muscular frame holding me tightly. I have pictured this hug for weeks now, craved it, daydreamed about it. I've missed him so much while he was finishing out the racing season.

"I'm the real present," Liam says, his lips pressed against the top of my head. "I hope that's okay."

"Seeing you is better than any physical gift," I say, dipping my head back to peer up at him.

"Is anyone home?" he asks, glancing behind me to where I've left the front door wide open.

I shake my head. "Mom's at work until six, and Brent is at college."

"Cool," he says, his smile timid. He doesn't have to say it because I already know – he hasn't met my mom yet, so if she were here, he'd have to meet her. And of course, the really big concern is my brother. But Brent's not here. We have the house to ourselves. Nothing is going to ruin this day.

I let him inside and thank him for the roses. "I didn't get you anything," I say, twisting my fingers together nervously. "I thought about it, but I wasn't supposed to see you today."

Liam runs his finger down the side of my chin, and then leans in for a quick kiss. "No worries, Bella. All I want is you. When I realized I could come home a day early, I knew I had to surprise you."

"Best surprise ever," I say.

I sit on the couch and pull him down next to me. I'm so happy he's here, that I can't help myself. I scoot closer to him on the couch until our bodies are pressed up against each other. Liam wraps an arm around me and tugs me even closer.

"Come here," he says, wrapping a hand around my feet and tugging them into his lap. Now I'm half sitting on the couch and half in his lap. "I missed you so much, I need more of you next to me."

I laugh and snuggle up with him, resting my head on his chest while his arms wrap protectively around me. I want to snuggle up here and stay here forever. But that might get awkward when my mom gets home from work. I should probably tell her about Liam soon. I haven't dated much in my life and I don't want her to walk in on me making out with some guy. I need to announce it to her in a better way.

"So, tell me all about it," I say. Even my voice sounds softer, happier, now that I'm with him. I feel like an entirely different person. Like someone with things to look forward to now. "How'd all of the leaving Team Loco stuff go?"

He exhales slowly. "Well, it was hard. That's for sure. I really love those guys on the team, and they've become like best friends to me over the months. Or like brothers, really. So that part sucked, but I know we'll stay friends."

"If they make Roca Springs MX into a national race track, then you'll get to see them once a year," I say. Our local dirt bike track has been getting scoped out by the industry professionals as a possible place to host a national race. It would be really cool to have that going on in my town, and the thousands of famous racers and fans would really boost the town's economy, not to mention how great it would be for the track owner.

"That would be cool," Liam says. "I basically spent the last week saying my goodbyes, turning in all my gear and stuff, and filming interviews."

"*More* interviews?" I say, rolling my eyes. "Man, these people love interviews."

"Yeah, tell me about it. But Marcus said it would help to dissolve any rumors about me before they started. Instead of just dropping off the team and never coming back, I could give an interview and tell everyone why I left, so no one could start some rumor saying I got in trouble, or anything nefarious. Now my reputation is clean."

I don't know why I feel so nervous to ask this question. I guess I'm afraid of what the answer might be, but I want to know it, so I ask, "What did you tell them was the reason you left?"

His tongue slides over his bottom lip, a quick gesture that makes me want to kiss him. He tightens his hold around me. "I told them I was eternally grateful for the opportunity Team Loco gave me to race professionally, but that my heart has changed, and I'd like to pursue other avenues in my career."

I laugh. "That's a very political answer."

"Yep," he says with a chuckle. "It sounds better than telling them the truth, which is that I just kind of hated professional racing, and that the entire thing was a total let down from what I spent my life believing it would be."

"Probably best that you didn't say that," I agree. "The fans love you and you don't want them to hate you."

"Totally. Plus, it's not like I'm done with motocross. I still plan on being at the track with you every chance we get."

It warms my heart to think about going to the track with Liam again, like how we used to last summer before he went pro. Those days were some of the best days of my life. Just me and Liam, the sun and the dirt bike track. Carefree, amazing days doing the sport I love. I need more of that in my life, especially since it makes me happy. Lately all I've been thinking about is how I'm now in my second semester of college and I have no idea what I want to be "when I grow up." How long can you go without knowing that kind of thing? I'm almost nineteen. I'm an adult. There's only so many more years until I'll officially be "all grown up" and I'll need a career by then.

But I refuse to think about that right now. Liam is here, I'm wrapped in his arms, and life is good.

"Want to watch some Netflix?" I say, reaching for the remote.

"Yes, but there's one more thing I need to do," Liam says.

"What's that?"

He grins and peers down at me. "Will you be my girlfriend?"

I feel my body flush from head to toe. It's such a simple, little kid type of question, but I think it's sweet that he asked. I nod, so excited and giddy that I'm having a hard time finding my voice.

"Yes," I manage to say after a moment. "I thought you'd never ask."

2

LIAM

It was seemingly overnight that my entire life changed. I went from living in Houston with my dad and training every day of my life to become a pro racer, to getting that dream, to giving it all up and falling for a girl in Roca Springs. Sure, it took eight months, but sometimes it feels like it was just a few hours. In my mind, I'm a brand-new person. I'm not that same guy who was completely obsessed with becoming a professional racer anymore. I'm different. My priorities are different. They're better. Much better.

I'm an adult now and I know what I want from this life. Family, my girl, and a career that won't keep me away from them. I've been getting my college degree online, and now that I'm settling down in one town for good, I've looked into switching to the local university. But if I keep my classes online, I'll probably be able to get a full-time job and do both of them. Just because I got that one big paycheck from Team Loco doesn't mean I can skip working. Taxes took a good chunk of that money, and college is taking another chunk of it. I want to work and save up for my own apartment. Maybe even a place that Bella would want to share with me one day.

I get home around six, having left Bella's house just in time to avoid meeting her mom. Bella assured me that she wants us to meet—and soon—but she wanted to tell her mom about me first. I know her mom will like me, but I worry about Brent. I'm enemy number one to him, and he's made it very clear that he wants me far away from his sister. Once he finds out we're officially dating... well, I don't even want to think about what will happen.

Back home, I find my little brothers playing Xbox very loudly in the living room. Phil is working on a proposal for his work, and my mom is standing in the guest room, which is now my room. Her hands are on her hips and she's just staring blankly.

"What's going on?" I ask.

"I'm trying to figure out where to begin," she says, looking around at all of the junk that's piled up. This room has a small twin bed up against the wall, and a desk and boxes of random stuff on the other side. It was their junk room before I moved in last summer.

"You don't have to clean out the room," I tell her. "I'm fine sleeping on the bed until I can get a job and get my own place."

Mom's lips press together. "Liam, you're perfectly welcome to stay here! I *want* you to stay here! Getting a job and an apartment would just be a waste of your money right now. Just focus on school and you can get a job after you graduate."

"School doesn't take that much time," I say. "I want a job. I want money. I want to contribute around here."

Mom rolls her eyes. "I appreciate that, I do. But you don't have to grow up so fast, son. Stay here and focus on school."

I'm not about to give up so easily. I have a girlfriend now and I want to spoil her like crazy. "What about a part time job?"

Mom rolls her eyes. "If you insist. Now help me move all this crap to the garage."

We get to work, hauling out every random thing that was hidden away in this room over the years. Mom insists that she and Phil are going to go through it in detail and throw most of it away, but Phil says that once things end up in the garage, they stay there forever. I tend to agree with him, but hey, their junk isn't my problem.

With everything out of the room, it looks much bigger. We even get rid of that god-awful twin bed. I thought about having my bed from home moved over here but it was a nightmare getting that thing up to our high-rise condo and it would be just as much of a nightmare getting it down. So, I decide to buy a new bed instead. Bella says she'd be happy to go bed shopping with me this afternoon, so I decide to swing by her house and pick her up. We can get dinner while we're at it. Bella insists on hitting up a food truck instead of a real restaurant because the Valentine's Day rush will have all the local places filled with wait lists. I love this new life of mine. Hanging out at home with my family in the day and going furniture shopping with Bella in the evening.

Now all I need to do is meet her mom and hope that it goes smoothly. My mom and Phil love Bella, but who could blame them? There's nothing to dislike about her. Bella has assured me that her mom will like me, too, but I'm not so sure. As soon as Brent finds out about our relationship, he's sure to put a stop to that. I'll have to meet her mom before Brent discovers that I'm dating his little sister. Maybe I can win her over so much that she won't let Brent's hatred of me put too much of a damper on things.

Speaking of meeting her mom, Bella tells me to pick her up in her driveway today. She hasn't had much time to tell her mom about us, and I get it. We haven't even been an official couple for twenty-four hours yet. Whenever I meet her, it needs to be a preplanned event so we can make sure she gets the best possible impression of me. Last night I barely slept because I spent the entire time worrying that her parents will trust Brent's hatred of me and force her to break up with me. I shudder at the memory as I drive toward her house.

Roca Springs is a small Texas town, the kind of small town where everyone knows everyone. My mom moved out here to get away from the big city. Now that I'm here, one of my favorite things about it is the lack of traffic. There are only a few stoplights in town, because most intersections just have a stop sign.

I'm cruising toward Bella's house, the radio cranked up, when I hear a loud sound of tires screeching. Then, up ahead, I see a truck get T-boned by a red Camaro. The truck was one car ahead of me, and our road has the green light. This idiot in the Camaro clearly ran his light. Smoke and the smell of burned rubber rises from the car crash in front of me. I slam on my brakes and pull over on the side of the road and call 911.

I report the accident to the dispatcher, who asks if there are any injuries. "Probably," I say, jogging up to the scene. A guy stumbles out of his Camaro, looking bewildered. As if he had no idea this kind of thing would happen if he ran a red light. What a moron. He could have killed himself.

With the phone still pressed to my ear, I jog over

to the truck that was smacked right on the driver's side. The windows are shattered, and the door is so caved in that there's no way to open it, even if the Camaro wasn't blocking it. I go to the passenger side and tug on the door. Luckily it opens.

"There's just one passenger in here," I tell the dispatcher.

"Emergency units are on the way," she says. I hang up the phone and shove it in my pocket.

"Hey, buddy, are you okay?" I call out to the driver, whose head is leaning against the steering wheel. Oh God, I hope he's not dead.

Then he moves. He's slow and unsteady as he coughs. He cries out in pain and reaches for his leg. "Help," he calls out, his voice strained.

"It's okay," I tell him as I lean into the passenger side of his truck. "An ambulance is on the way."

He looks over at me. Blood pours from his forehead and his jaw. His eyes are wide and fluttery, and his expression looks like he probably suffered a concussion. "Help," he stutters out. "My...leg...oh god the pain...holy--" He inhales a sharp breath through his teeth. "Oh god, it hurts."

I look down and see that his left leg is crushed between the truck and the door that was caved in from the impact. Even from here, there's a bend in his leg that shouldn't be there. My stomach twists anxiously as my mind races for all the knowledge I know about first aid. Should I help him? Should I leave him in case moving him causes more injury? I don't know. But I should definitely keep him talking so he doesn't lose consciousness.

"Hey man, look at me," I call out. "It's going to be okay."

He groans in pain. Blood drips from his head onto the leather seats.

"What's your name?" I say, just for something to keep him talking.

He looks over at me now, really looks over. I see him head on, and our eyes meet, and a curse word escapes my lips. I can't believe I didn't notice it before, but in the panic of the moment, I had only cared about calling 911 and making sure he was okay. My brain didn't even register that I know this guy, not until now.

And the look in his eyes says he notices it too.

"It's going to be okay," I say again. In the distance, the wail of an ambulance siren is a welcome sound. "They're almost here."

I take a step back.

"Wait," Brent calls out. His expression is twisted in pain, his chest heaving with each breath. There's a desperation in his eyes, one I think anyone would have if they were trapped in a car and confused and probably suffering from a concussion. This is the first time he's looked at me without venom in his gaze. Instead, his eyes are pleading with me. "Don't leave."

"I won't," I promise. Then I wait with Bella's brother until the ambulance arrives.

3

BELLA

I shiver as a burst of chilly wind slams into me. This is a fairly cold Valentine's Day for Texas, and here I am sitting outside in it, freezing my butt off while I wait on my brand-new boyfriend who is running late. Warning signs are flashing in my mind, bright and bold and terrifying. I keep thinking, if Liam is my boyfriend now, why is he late picking me up? According to the text on my phone, he said he was on his way over forty-five minutes ago. It only takes about ten minutes to get from his house to mine.

I'm starting to feel a little stood up. Panic threatens to take over my thoughts, as I sit here cold and bored and alone, wondering if maybe this whole thing was a joke. If Liam was just going to make me think he wanted to date me and then he'd show up with his friends and yell, "sike!" and they'd all laugh at me.

Deep down, I know this can't possibly be true. Liam is a great guy. He cares about me.

So why is he late?

I stare out at the setting sun as it dips below my neighbor's house across the street. My phone rings, and I jump. I'm so glad Liam's name is on the caller ID or I might scream. The last thing I want to do is get a call from some random person.

"Hello?" I answer, trying not to sound accusatory in my voice, but I am pretty upset.

"Bella, you and your mom need to get to the hospital," he says. His voice is strained, like he's been running a marathon or something.

I stand up on the porch. "What? Why?"

"It's Brent," he says. I hear his truck door close, and the sounds of his keys jamming into the ignition. "He's been in a wreck."

"What?" I can barely understand the words I'm hearing. Why on earth would Liam be calling me about my brother, who he tries to stay very far away from?

Then I hear it. An ambulance siren pierces through the phone, and reality jolts into me. Liam's words all make sense now. Brent was in a wreck.

"Is he okay?" I ask as I turn and practically crash through my front door. "What happened?"

"He's okay," Liam says quickly, his voice calmer.

He must hear the panic in my voice and is trying to calm me down. "He'll be okay. I was driving to your house and I saw a car run a red light and hit him. He's got a broken leg and he's a little out of it, but he's okay. They're taking him to Clear Springs Hospital right now."

"Oh my God." My eyes blur slightly, and I blink to make them go right again. My heart is pounding. The thought of something bad happening to my brother is making me all flustered. I look around the room, realizing Mom isn't in here. "Mom?" I call out.

"I'm following the ambulance," Liam says. "Just drive safely and get here as soon as you can. I'll be there waiting on you."

"Okay," I say, and I hang up the phone.

Mom is in her bedroom, wearing a robe, with a towel wrapped around her wet hair. Her eyes widen when she sees me. "Get dressed! You have to get dressed. We have to go!"

I rush to her closet and start yanking out shirts and tossing them at her.

"Holy crap, Bella," Mom says. "Whoa, slow down." She grabs my arms. "What is going on?"

I take a deep breath. It's just a broken leg and some mild confusion, I remind myself. It's not like he's about to drop dead or anything. "Brent was just in a car wreck. I guess he was going to come home for the weekend or something—he has a broken leg and he's being taken to the hospital right now."

Mom doesn't say anything; she just jumps into action. She takes some clothes and goes into her bathroom, emerging a few seconds later dressed in yoga pants and a Roca Springs PTA shirt. She throws her wet hair into a bun on top of her head and slips her feet into some flip flops.

"I'll drive," she says.

We park at the emergency room, right next to Liam's truck. I'm happy to see that only one other person is sitting in here waiting to be seen, so hopefully Brent will get care immediately. The thought of my brother laying here in pain does not sit well with me.

Mom rushes to the counter to talk to the nurses. I spot Liam sitting in a chair and I walk over to him. He stands up and I crash into him, wrapping my arms around him instinctively. He holds me a long time.

"I thought you were going to stand me up for dinner," I say, finally pulling away once the nervous pain in my chest lightens a bit.

He gives me a slow, soft grin. "Never. Everything was just so urgent that I wasn't able to call you right away. I waited with Brent until the paramedics arrived. I couldn't do anything but stand there because he was crushed against the truck door."

"Oh my God," my mom says.

I jump, not realizing she's here, standing right

next to us. How long has she been here? Did she see me hug him? Oh crap. *Oh, crap, oh crap.*

"So, someone hit him?" Mom asks.

Liam nods. "A Camaro. Some young guy was driving, and he completely ran the red light. I gave a witness statement to the police at the scene. That guy wasn't injured but the police detained him. I hope he gets his license taken away."

"I hope so, too," Mom says. She glances toward the double doors that lead into the hospital. "The nurses told me a doctor will come talk with me soon. You said Brent is stable, right?"

Liam nods. "He's okay. They rushed him back as soon as the ambulance arrived."

"Good," Mom says. She glances at me. "Do you want to introduce me to your friend?"

I feel my cheeks redden. "This is, um, Liam."

He holds out his hand. "Nice to meet you."

"You too," Mom says, smiling at him. "I'm so glad you were there. Who knows how long they would have taken to call us."

I know this isn't the right time, not by a long shot, but I'm kind of tired of keeping things from my mom. I kept the entire summer fling away from everyone, only telling Kylie once it was over. I'm sick of living my life in the shadows, having this amazing relationship and not telling anyone about it.

"Liam is my boyfriend," I blurt out.

"Well, why didn't you say so earlier?" Mom says.

She looks at Liam now, seemingly impressed with what she sees. "He's cute, that's for sure."

"It's still new," I say, looking at Liam. He looks just as uncomfortable as I feel. "He... He just asked me to be his girlfriend earlier today."

"On Valentine's Day," Mom says, grinning. "How sweet. Well, it's nice to meet you, Liam."

I am freaked out and awkward but also relieved to finally have this news out in the open. The double doors swing outward and a doctor dressed in light green scrubs looks around, eyes landing on my mom. "Brent Castro's family?"

"That's us," Mom says, rushing over to him.

The doctor tells us that Liam suffered a pretty severe leg break, and that they are taking him into surgery now. He'll need pins and screws to secure his leg back together, but he'll have a full recovery. He also has a pretty severe concussion that will probably cause him pain for a month or two, and he had to get stitches on his forehead and arm. But overall, he's okay.

We hang out in the emergency room waiting area for two hours while Brent is in surgery. I tell Liam he's free to go home, but he insists on staying with me. He goes to the hospital's cafeteria and brings back dinner for the three of us, and it all goes pretty well as far as waiting in a hospital waiting room goes.

Finally, my brother is out of surgery and awake

from the anesthesia. Mom and I go back there to see him. He's a little loopy looking, with bandages over his fresh stitches, but overall, he's doing pretty well. He could have died in a wreck like that.

"Heyyyyy," he says, his head lopping to the side when we walk in his room. "I feel funny."

"Well you look awful," I say with a smile.

Mom runs her hand gingerly over his cheek. He might be in his early twenties, but he's still her child. "I'm so glad you're okay," she says.

"My workouts are going to be screwed," he says with a frown as he looks down at his leg. "Hopefully I can still do upper body while I'm waiting on this thing to heal."

"Just focus on getting better," Mom says. "Workouts can wait until later."

Brent scoffs. My brother is basically a muscle man. He could pose for a protein shake advertisement if he wanted. All he cares about is college work and working out at the gym. As far as I know, he hasn't really dated since Samantha broke his heart all those years ago.

"Do you remember anything about the wreck?" I ask him.

He studies me for a while, his thoughts taking a long time to form in his mind. He's on a ton of painkillers right now, so I wonder how much he'll remember once they wear off. Finally, Brent says, "I remember your boy was there."

Chills prickle over my skin. Here it comes. He's going to tell Mom how much he hates Liam, and my very first day of being his official girlfriend will be tainted with another family argument.

"Yeah," I say, my voice weak. "He's in the waiting room right now."

Brent takes a slow breath, his eyelids fluttering with the last remnants of the anesthesia. "I guess he's not so bad," my brother murmurs before closing his eyes and drifting off to sleep.

"We should let him rest," Mom says, patting my arm as she stands up. I walk back to the waiting room in a daze. My brother just said the nicest thing he's ever said about Liam. He'll probably completely change his mind once we're back home and the pain meds have worn off, but that doesn't change the fact that he said it this time.

Today has truly been a surprising day. I don't even want to know what tomorrow will bring.

4

LIAM

I spend the next two days fixing up my new bedroom at home. I ended up going bed shopping with my mom instead of Bella because she was with her brother in the hospital. I got a simple platform bed and a comfortable mattress to go with it. I let my mom pick out the sheets, and she chose gray and black sheets with a matching comforter. So long as it's soft, I don't really care what it looks like. I also got a dresser and a TV stand. I brought my TV from my old room at my dad's, as well as most of my clothes and stuff that I'll need while I'm living here.

I was a little worried that my dad might get offended at me moving out of his place, but if anything, he seemed relieved about it. I think that's because my dad dates a lot of women and never wanted to bring them home if I was going to be there. Now he's free to do as he pleases, and I'm getting to live the family life I've grown to love.

On Sunday morning, after two nights in the hospital, Bella calls to tell me that Brent is going home. They had kept him for observation with his head, but he's going to be okay. She says he has a migraine but he's in decent spirits, and is only complaining about how he can't hit the gym or ride his dirt bike for a while.

I've only talked to Bella on the phone in the last twenty four hours because it felt weird if I were to hang around the hospital now that Brent had a room. I don't exactly want to see him right now because I know what once I do, that happy bubble of new relationship joy will burst like a balloon with a needle poked at it.

This isn't exactly how I pictured my first few days of dating Bella, but I guess life loves throwing curveballs at us. A year ago, all I cared about was motocross. Now, all I care about is Bella.

I'm hanging out in the living room while my brothers play Xbox later in the day. I'm on my laptop, trying to find local places that are hiring for part time jobs. The bad thing about small towns like Roca Springs is that most of the local businesses don't maintain decent websites, and they certainly don't post job openings to job websites. I'll have to go around in person to see if anyone is hiring.

When Bella calls, I can't help but smile before I

answer the phone. I can't wait until her life gets normal again so we can start spending every second together. I still owe her that dinner date we didn't get to go on.

"Hey," I say, answering the phone. I stop myself before adding the word beautiful just because my brothers are within earshot and they will absolutely start making kissing sounds if they know I'm talking to Bella. "How's it going?"

"Brent is home and he's doing okay. He's refusing to use the wheelchair my mom borrowed from our neighbor. He wants to just hop around on one foot like an idiot. I told him he's going to hurt himself even more like that."

I chuckle. "Sounds like something I would do. It sucks not being mobile."

Bella sighs into the phone. "I miss you."

I glance at my brothers, who seem pretty occupied by the game. "I miss you more," I say softly.

"Do you want to come over?"

"Why don't you come over here?" I ask.

"I would, but I want to be here in case my mom needs help with helping Brent. *Pleaseee* come over." I can tell she's using that cute pleading voice of hers to win me over.

"What if it's… awkward?" I say.

"Who cares? It's not like Brent can get up and try to fight you right now," she says with a laugh. "He's going to have to get over it eventually. We're dating and there's nothing he can do about it."

I really, really, don't want to see her brother right now. "There might not be anything he can do about it, but there's definitely things he can say about it."

"Please?" she says. And just like that, I'm agreeing. I can't say no to her, especially not when she uses that voice.

Before going to Bella's house, I stop by a local food truck and pick up a bunch of tacos and some chips and salsa. Maybe it'll help ease some of the tension in the room if I bring food. I mean, everyone loves tacos.

Bella opens the door before I knock. She must have been watching for me out of the window.

"I brought food," I say, holding up the heavy paper bag.

"Oooh," her mom says from the other side of the room. "Is that tacos?"

"Yes ma'am."

"Perfect!" she says. "Oh Liam, I like you."

From across the room, Brent scoffs.

"Don't worry about him," Bella tells me as she lets me inside. "He's a grump."

I see Brent laying in the recliner in the living room, his leg in a soft cast. He's flipping the channels on the TV remote and not looking at me, probably purposely avoiding me.

I wonder if he remembers how he'd asked me to

stay with him when he was stuck in his truck. I know better than to bring that up, though. He was delirious and in a lot of pain. He would have asked anyone to stay.

We all settle around the TV and eat my taco peace offering. I'm glad Brent eats the tacos Bella hands him and doesn't try to do some boycotting of me by refusing. He ignores us for the most part.

I think the fact that Bella's mom is in the room makes him keep his thoughts to himself. I hope she never leaves.

"Isn't it lucky that Liam happened to see your wreck happen?" she says after a solid fifteen minutes of peaceful eating. Crap. Beside me, Bella tenses.

"Yeah it was cool," Bella says quickly. "Let's watch the show."

"You've seen this show a million times," her mom says. "I just want to thank Liam again. He was a real help by calling 911 and making sure Brent was okay."

"Probably the only decent thing he's ever done," Brent mutters under his breath, his gaze still on the television.

"What's that mean?" Bella's mom says. She turns to me. "Do you two know each other?"

"It's nothing," Bella says. "They used to race dirt bikes together. No big deal. Now, let's watch the show."

"Oh, how cool!" her mom says.

"Not cool," Brent mutters.

Her mom gives him a look. "What got your britches in a knot?"

"Mom, it's nothing." Bella is trying so hard to change the subject and avoid having her brother say something that will ruin everything. Normally I'd agree with her, but honestly, I'm sick of this feud. I didn't do anything wrong.

I set my soda down on the coaster on the coffee table. "Brent hates me," I say, which gets me a startled look from everyone in the room. "It's not because we used to race together. It's because a long time ago, his girlfriend found me at the races and told me she was single and then she kissed me. Brent found out, and he blames me for their relationship ending even though I didn't pursue her. She pursued me."

Bella is completely frozen.

Brent is too, his jaw ridged as he stares at me.

The only person to move is their mom. "Samantha?" she says, sounding like she doesn't want to believe it. She turns to Brent. "Is that what happened with you and Samantha?"

"Yeah," Brent says, looking down at his broken leg. "He's telling the truth about what happened, but I'm not so sure I believe his motives."

"I swear I didn't know," I say.

His mom looks at me and then back at Brent. "It

sounds like an honest mistake, honey. If Samantha did that to you, she wasn't worth dating anyway."

Brent just grumbles and shrugs his shoulders.

Bella finally finds her voice. "That's what I said. I told him he should hate her, not Liam."

"You should really consider forgiving him," her mom says. "It'll make things easier on your sister."

Brent looks over at me, and then looks back at the TV. "I'll think about it."

Bella's eyes widen and she grabs my hand. Nothing has really changed between her brother and me, but maybe… maybe with time, it will.

5

BELLA

I should have known that nothing fun and amazing could happen to me without it being laced with awkward, uncontrollable events. I am so giddy and elated that Liam is back home and that he's mine. All mine.

But of course, life had to throw a curveball at me and make Brent get hurt. The last few days have been so weird. My brother is basically living on the recliner in the living room now since he can't sleep well in his bed with the cast on his leg. That means he's always around. When I'm coming home or going out, he's there, watching me. Judging me. He doesn't say anything, but I know what he's thinking. He's mad that I'm dating Liam, but he doesn't want to admit that he lost this battle and I won it. Even our mom took my side instead of his. All I can do is hope that he eventually gets over it. I want my relationship with Liam to become the real deal.

Date nights, shopping trips, boring stuff, and fun stuff. I want him invited over for holidays and random pizza nights. I want him to sit with my family when I graduate college. If Brent doesn't just suck it up and get over his anger with Liam, then all of those events will be awkward.

I'm sitting in my government class at the college, hanging out in the back row like some kind of loner. I don't have any friends in this class, so I've taken to sitting back here and texting Kylie when I should probably be listening to the lecture. Government is incredibly boring, or at least it is the way this guy teaches it. All he does is talk about politics and try to get the class all riled up about the current state of things. Unfortunately, which candidate you love or hate the most is *not* on the final exam.

I text Kylie about how stressed I am about this whole Brent breaking his leg and being home thing.

Kylie: This might actually be a blessing in disguise.

Me: How so?

Kylie: Well, Liam was there for Brent when he had a moment of weakness. He was scared and inured, and he wanted Liam to stay with him. That kind of thing bonds people

Me: I think he was just delirious. My brother will never be friends with Liam

Kylie: Never say never!

When class is over, I scoop up my things and head out toward the student center that's across campus. I have two and a half hours to kill before my next class. It's not that far to drive home, but I'd rather just hang out here and get some lunch.

My head is down as I walk, still texting Kylie. Someone clears their throat in that obvious way like they're trying to get you to notice them. I look up.

"Liam!"

He's leaning against the wall next to the doors that lead to the student center. I swear he's standing like that on purpose, because it's how every sexy guy stands in the movies. All casual and laid back and effortlessly gorgeous.

"I thought you weren't going to notice me," he says, scooping me into his arms for a quick kiss.

"I didn't think there would be anyone *to* notice," I say, putting my phone in my bag. "What are you doing here?"

"I just thought I'd surprise my favorite person and hang out with them for lunch. This is the day you have some time to kill before your next class, right?"

I love that he pays attention to the random things I say. I nod. "Are you hungry? They have a pretty good toasted club sandwich here."

"Baby, I'm always hungry," Liam says, pulling

open the door with one hand and reaching for my hand with the other. "Lead the way."

The student center is the newest part of the community college. The building was built two years ago, and it was a way for the school to make itself look more attractive to prospective students. It's a large, octagonal-shaped building with mostly glass walls. There's a café that serves pretty decent food, and an eating area that overlooks the manmade pond in front of the campus. I like to grab a snack and sit next to the windows, watching the ducks splash around in the lake.

Across from the café are lounge rooms with brightly colored sofas and pool tables, air hockey, and other games. I haven't ventured in there yet. There's also the student store and some meeting rooms where people host the various clubs around campus.

The whole building this this modern, sleek feel to it that reminds me of Liam's old condo he shared with his dad.

"You know what this place reminds me of?" I say, turning to him.

"A Mosely International original?"

"No way. Your dad made this?"

He nods. "Oh yeah. This has my dad's architecture style written all over it. I remember him talking about it a while back. There are a lot of his designs in small Texas towns like these."

"How did he take the news that you were moving out?" I ask as we make our way to the line to order food.

Liam shrugs. "He didn't care. If anything, I think he was relieved. Now he can get up to all kinds of single man debauchery without worrying if I'll be home."

My eyes widen, and he laughs. "I'm playing. My dad's not a weirdo. At least I don't think he is."

We order our food and Liam whips out his wallet. "I can pay for mine," I say.

"Nope. You're my girlfriend and I want to pay."

"That's sexist," I say.

"No, it's not. I didn't say you're not allowed to pay... I said I want to pay."

"Let him pay, honey," the cashier says. She's an older woman with graying hair and smile lines. "If there's one thing I've learned after three divorces, it's to take the romance where you can find it."

Now I feel completely awkward. I glance at Liam. "Fine, but I'm paying next time."

"Fine, but I'll argue with you next time too," he says, giving me a wink before handing the woman his debit card.

I love how effortless our relationship is. I love that he's sweet and fun and surprises me at school just to have lunch. It's only been a few days, but Liam is the best boyfriend I've ever had.

We get our food and I lead him to my favorite table with the best view of the ducks.

"So how is college life treating you?" he asks.

A few tables over, there are two girls staring at us, and I recognize the look on their faces. They think Liam is too hot to be real. I can also detect some jealousy in their stares. They're probably hoping I'm his sister or cousin or something. Too bad, ladies. He's all mine.

I grin, and then remember his question. "It's okay. Mostly boring. How are your online classes?"

"Totally boring." He takes a bite of his sandwich and nods. "This is good."

"Told you," I say, reaching for my bag of chips. I open it and dump them all on top of the paper container next to my sandwich. "I guess no one ever promised that college would be fun," I say.

"That's for sure. Maybe if you're in a frat or something…"

"Do you want to be in a frat?" I ask.

He snorts. "No way. I love my life the way it is." His gaze lingers on mine, and I feel that warm feeling squeezing around my heart. I know without a doubt that Liam and I are the real deal.

"So, what are you going to do once you graduate college?" I ask.

He shrugs. "I'll figure something out."

"Doesn't that freak you out?"

He takes a huge bite of his food. "What?"

I look out at the ducks, and I kind of wish my life was that easy. Swim around a lake, eat pieces of bread that people toss at you. What a carefree life.

"You're not freaked out that you have no plan?"

"I do have a plan," he says. "I'm going to get a part time job, keep taking classes, and graduate in two years."

"That's not really a long-term plan…" All the trepidation I feel about my life is swallowing me whole. I can't believe Liam is so calm about it. "What do you want to do with your career? Your entire adult life?"

His lips slide into a grin. "Baby, I have time to figure that out. I'll probably land somewhere in the motocross realm. Maybe I'll manage my own race team one day. I don't know. We're young. We can figure it out."

"I wish I was that laid back about it."

His head tilts to the side. "What's wrong?"

I shrug. "I have no idea what I want to do. And it's massively freaking me out. Like… panic attacks once a week freaking me out."

"Baby…" Liam's voice is soothing as he reaches across the table and puts his hand on top of mine. "Just breathe, okay? You're only eighteen."

"Nineteen soon," I say.

"You're only nineteen soon," he says with a sneaky grin. He squeezes my hand. "I promise we'll find something you want to do with your life. I mean, we've found each other so that's one big ball of amazing. Right? We've got each other, so we've got this."

I'm not convinced. I mean, yeah, I'm so happy to be Liam's girlfriend. Beyond happy. But that's not a future. I don't think my mom planned on becoming a department store manager when she was younger. She just worked there after school and then got a promotion and another one and another one until somehow she was the boss at the same place she's worked her whole life. That's not exactly a passion.

I want a passion.

"This is really bothering you, isn't it?" Liam's chocolatey eyes are concerned as he watches me.

I nod.

"Well, that won't do," he says, sitting up straighter. "I'm making it my personal mission to find your dream career."

I lift an eyebrow. "How exactly are you going to do that? I've already taken a ton of career tests online and they're all stupid."

He waves his hand, dismissing my idea. "Tests are stupid. Real life isn't. We're going to go out and try every job there is until something sparks a fire in you."

I give him a look. "I'm not sure that's going to work."

Liam shakes his head. "Oh, it'll work. I'm not going to stop until you're happy." He lets go of my hand and reaches for his sandwich again. "We'll figure this out, baby, I promise."

I'm not so sure he's right. Sure, his heart is in the right place, but I'm pretty sure I'm doomed when it comes to finding a fun career.

But there's one thing I am sure about: I love it when he calls me baby. I'm really loving this whole boyfriend-girlfriend thing. It's a million times better than a summer fling.

6

LIAM

*B*ella has always been so focused. That's one of the many things I like about her. When she first met me, she got angry and decided I was a terrible person. It took a lot of work on my part to convince her otherwise. When I started giving her some motocross lessons just for fun, she took them seriously. She listened to every word I said and did her best to implement them and it really worked. Her skills improved so much that she's nearly unrecognizable on the track now.

So, it really bothers me to hear that she's been stressing out about the future. I don't want her to be afraid of the months and years to come, to feel like she doesn't have a plan. If she's worried about her life in the future, then that means she's worried about us, too. I don't want her future to feel like a vast cavern of emptiness. I want her to be excited for it. For us. For the future we can build together, now that we're an official couple.

When she confided in me earlier today at the college, she also struck a small chord deep inside of me. It made me think about my own life. I don't exactly have my future planned out, either. For so long, all I cared about was going pro. Then that happened and I tossed it aside, setting my sights on a better horizon. And I'm here now, and I love my life as it currently is. Sure, I'd like a job, and I'm sure I'll get one soon. I also need to finish college, but that'll happen, too. After that? Well, it hadn't ever bothered me until now.

I push those thoughts to the back of my mind. I know I'll land somewhere, and it'll be great. Right now, I'm worried about Bella. I promised I'd help her find her dream career today. I know she didn't exactly believe me, but I'm not about to let my words become an empty promise.

When I get home after leaving Bella to her last class of the day, I find my mom in the kitchen chopping up vegetables and putting them in the slow cooker. I sit on a nearby barstool and watch her work. She's an excellent cook. I tried cooking a thing or two over the summer when I lived here, but I am definitely no skilled chef, unlike my mom. Her movements are precise, measured. She's been cooking dinner a long time and it shows.

"Hey, Mom?"

"Yes?" she says, not looking up from her task.

"Have you always wanted to be a stay at home mom?"

Now she looks up. "Why do you ask?"

"Bella is freaking out about how she doesn't know what she wants to do with her life. I'm trying to help her come up with career ideas."

Mom reaches for an onion and slices it in half. "When I was your age, I didn't know what I wanted to do with my life, that's for sure. All I cared about was friends and parties and boys. I knew I wasn't going to college because my parents couldn't afford it." She puts the onion into the slow cooker and shrugs. "I guess I didn't really have a plan, either. I met your father and we got married just a couple of months later. Then you were born. I stayed home to take care of you, and well, that's how it's always been. I was seriously thinking about getting a job during those few years when I was divorced and single. The money I got from the divorce held me over, but I was bored. I applied at a couple of daycares."

"Really?" I say. "I didn't know you wanted to work at a daycare."

Mom smiles. "I just love kids. I wanted to work with them. But then I met Phil and he had the sweetest little boys..." She glances back toward the hallway, then looks at me. "Sorry, son. I'm not really much help in the career department."

"Maybe Bella would like to be a stay at home mom."

Mom's eyes widen.

"If and when we have kids," I say quickly, just so she doesn't get any ideas.

Mom studies me for a moment. "You really think you and Bella are the real deal?"

I nod. "Of course I do. Why? Don't you?"

"You're both very young," Mom says, turning her attention back to the stew she's making. "I love Bella dearly. It's you I'm worried about."

"I'm offended," I say playfully. "But seriously, why?"

"I just worry that you'll miss motocross and want to go back to it. I don't want you breaking her heart, son, but I also know how it is to be young and in love. Things change. You grow up, you move on. Your hearts want different things… I don't think you should worry too much about the future. Just live in the moment."

"I'm not going to change my mind. Professional motocross didn't make me happy, but Bella does."

My mom smiles. "Then I don't think you two have anything to worry about.

I WAKE UP THE NEXT MORNING FILLED WITH anticipation and a sense of purpose. I spent all night last night looking up careers and trying to decide if Bella would like them. In some ways, it feels like I know her so well, and in other ways, I'm reminded that I don't. We haven't even spent a full year together yet. I still have so much to learn about this girl that I'm crazy about.

My research wasn't totally fruitless, though. I came across a ton of career options that sound both interesting, and like they'd be something Bella likes. I'm not too sure about the first one on my list, but it was the quickest event I could arrange for tonight. Instead of just showing her a list of possible careers or looking up YouTube videos on them and hoping something sounds interesting to her, I have a brilliant idea. I'm going to give her a hands-on experience. She just doesn't know it yet.

Bella's mom answers the door when I arrive at her house. "Well hello," she says, stepping back and letting me inside. "Bella tells me you've planned some kind of secret for her."

"More like an adventure."

Bella emerges from the hallway, her smile getting brighter when she sees me. "Mom, I'm off to find my dream career," she says. "Whatever that might be."

"You two have fun," her mom says. She doesn't question the whole career thing. Like my own mom, Bella's mom probably thinks we're stressing too much about this. But I don't care. If it makes my girl happy, it's what I'm going to do.

Bella always gives me this look when I open the passenger door of my truck for her. It's like she's impressed? Or maybe I'm just thinking too much about it. I smile at her and she smiles back and then I close the door after she gets in my truck. Once I'm inside, she turns to me while buckling her seatbelt.

"Okay, show me the list."

"What list?" I ask, turning on the heater because she's shivering.

"The list you made of careers you think I'll like. I want to see if it's anything new I haven't thought of."

I give her a wry grin as I back out of her driveway. "Oh, there's no list. I'm way more fun than a stupid list."

Actually, there is a list at home. I wrote down all the ideas I came up with, but I'm not going to bring it and show it to her. That defeats the whole purpose of what I'm trying to do. Anything can look boring or exciting on paper. It's real life where you find out exactly what it is. With racing professionally, I had only ever thought about it as a kid. It seemed amazing. In reality? Not so much.

If all goes according to plan, over the next few weeks, I'll take her on several career-oriented adventures. And maybe she'll find something she wants to do and then she won't be so stressed out. I drive us across town to a little bakery I've never been to. But they have a website and it looks like a pretty legit place. The owner was even on some TV show baking contest a few years back and she won.

"Oooh, cupcakes," Bella says, her eyes sparkly as she gazes up at the neon sign that spells out Aunt Sally's Bakery. "Am I going to see if I'd like to be a professional cupcake taster?" she teases. "Because I already know I'd be good at that."

"We're doing something cooler than that," I say, meeting her in front of my truck. I open the door to the bakery and it's clear that there's an event going on here tonight. All the tables and chairs have been set up as little work stations. The whole place smells like sugar, and pastel colors are everywhere you look.

"Welcome!" a woman says. Her nametag says she's Aunt Sally, but she looks too young to be someone's aunt. "Let me guess," she says, looking at both of us. "You must be my date night couple? Liam and Bella?"

"That's us," I say, grinning when Bella gives me a surprised look.

"Let me show you your table," Aunt Sally says. She brings us to one of the tables, which has our names on it. There are other people sitting at the other tables, most of them alone, and middle aged. One table has what looks like a mother-daughter team on it. Oh well. I'm not too manly to play with cupcakes.

"What is this?" Bella says, running her fingers across the plastic tools that are laid out on our table.

I grin. "It's an introduction to cake decorating. Let me tell you, if you decide to own a bakery one day, I will fully support that." I pat my stomach. "All the free cupcakes and pastries I could ever want."

She laughs and takes a seat next to me.

Aunt Sally stands in the middle of everyone and smiles warmly at us. "Welcome to my third ever cake decorating workshop! I'm so glad to see so many new faces here! Tonight, we'll be decorating cupcakes and a mini cake that I've already baked for us, so the boring part is out of the way."

Some people chuckle at her joke. Two employees emerge from the back, carrying trays of naked cupcakes and cakes. They set a bunch down at every table and then Aunt Sally starts explaining every decorating tool and what it's used for. She promises we'll be able to make a perfect icing rose before the night is over.

Bella looks over at me, and whispers, "Thank you."

I kiss her forehead. And then, with Aunt Sally's careful instructions to guide our hands, we start decorating some cupcakes.

7

BELLA

The sterile smell of the hospital kind of freaks me out. I was here just a couple of weeks ago with Brent. That night everything was frantic, and I was filled with unknown worries about my brother. That smell made me nauseated while Mom and I waited in the emergency room for updates about my brother. The biggest memory I have from that night is the way the place smelled. It's not really a bad smell, just all clean and antiseptic.

Today, the same smell washes over me again as we enter the hospital. It's like when you take a dog to the vet and they get all freaked out about being there, even if it's just for a checkup. I know I'm not here because of some terrifying emergency, but the smell still gets to me.

"What are we doing today?" I ask Liam as he walk up to the front desk. At least we're in the main entrance and not the emergency room part today. "Brain surgery?"

"Do you want to be a brain surgeon?" he asks, playfully bumping into me as we walk.

"I don't think so." I curl my lip. "The idea of all that med school and having to cut open brains is just gross. But I'm grateful that some people are brave enough to do the job."

"Let's hope we never need brain surgery," he says.

At the front desk, Liam asks for Nurse Quintana. When she arrives, she's wearing bright pink lipstick that matches her pink Hello Kitty scrubs. She smells like candy and spearmint gum and she looks like one of those people who are always in a great mood.

"Hi there!" She shakes our hands. "Are you ready to get bloody?"

My eyes widen, and she bursts out in a grin. "Just a joke of my profession," she says, winking at Liam as she walks us to the elevators. "Actually, I say it all the time, but people hardly laugh."

"What is your job title?" I ask.

"I'm a blood bank technician," she says, punching the button for the seventh floor. "I started out as a nurse right after high school, but I didn't like all the bad parts of nursing. So, I went back and got my associates for this."

"You only need an associate degree?" I ask. "That's not bad."

"Not bad at all," Nurse Quintana says. "Two quick

years of med classes and then you're good to go. My starting salary was sixty-five thousand, but now I'm up to eighty."

"That's an amazing salary." I glance at Liam. "What made you think I'd like to be a blood bank technician?"

The nurse answers for him with a chuckle. "The poor thing called up here asking about different jobs you could shadow. My sister in law is actually the receptionist, so she got your phone call," she says to Liam. "She told me she recommends my job to everyone she knows because I make it sound so fun."

Liam shrugs. "The medical field is huge, and I figured you wouldn't want to be a surgeon or anything, but we had to stop by at least one medical job, just to see if you'd like it."

"Cool," I say. "Not working with sick people is a definite bonus."

Nurse Quintana nods. "Oh yeah, no worries there. Sometimes I never see patients. It's just me and the nurses and the rest of my coworkers."

We get off on the seventh floor and she shows me the lab where she works. There are locked cases of blood everywhere. She explains to me that her main job is to categorize and keep inventory of all the blood the hospital has on hand. When a patient comes in needing a transfusion, they're responsible for finding compatible blood and dispensing it to the doctors. It's a pretty laid-back work environment, and she gets her own office. Plus, it would be cool to wear scrubs all day, especially if I can get some featuring my favorite cartoon characters.

"So, what did you think?" Liam asks when we're walking back to his truck an hour later.

"It was cool, but it doesn't feel like a dream job," I admit. "I'm not sure I'd want to be at a hospital all day."

"I get that," he says. "I have a good feeling about our next stop."

"We're going to another place?" I ask.

He grins. "Yep. I have made a lot of phone calls in the last few days."

We get on the main street that goes through town and I wonder exactly how many job shadowing adventures my new boyfriend has set up for me. "You are seriously too amazing to be real," I say.

Liam pinches his arm. "And yet… I am."

"Did you know back in the summer?" I ask.

He glances at me briefly while we pull up to a stop sign. "Did I know what?"

"That we would be officially together one day?"

He blows air out of his lips. "Nope. I wanted it though. I think I had told myself from day one of our summer fling that you were unattainable. You felt like a prize I'd never actually get."

My chest floods with warm, mushy feelings. I don't even know how to reply to that. It's so sweet it makes my heart hurt.

"Here we are," Liam says, putting on his turn signal.

I look out the window and see our county's animal shelter. I can't help but grin. "Oh, I think I'm going to like this job."

Liam has signed us up to play with the dogs at the shelter. They need at least an hour of playtime a day, but more if there's enough volunteers for it. We sign in and get nametags and the woman at the front counter tells us she's grateful that we're here because they haven't had volunteers all week.

I ask her a few job-specific questions, and she tells me there's no special college degree needed for her job. She's the only day shift crew member, and there are three other part-timers as well as someone who stays overnight with the animals. Since the animal shelter is founded by tax dollars, and the city is always cutting the budget, they don't earn much money. That part kind of totally sucks. But playing with the dogs is so much fun.

Liam and I take a few dogs out of their pens at a time and go outside to the fenced in yard where they can run and play. We play fetch and chase and get tackled with furry, smelly dog kisses. By the end of it, we're both sweating, and we smell like dogs ourselves. But it's so, so very much fun.

I talk to the woman who works here, and her name is Beth. She's been here for twelve years, and she told me it took her five years just to get the job because there's so few opportunities and people tend to stay until they retire. Unfortunately, that's exactly what she plans to do. So, unless I want to move far away and find another animal shelter employee that's on the verge of retiring, I might be out of luck with this type of job.

Liam and I look up vet technicians and put them on the list of things to try out. I'd still get to work with animals in a job like that but seeing sick and hurt animals might be too sad for me.

We end up staying for three and a half hours. After playing with all of the dogs, we also play with the cats who are nice enough to want company. Some of them are grouchy and prefer that we just stay away from them. Those cats remind me of my brother. He's been a grumpy mess since his car accident. The prescription painkillers don't seem to help much, and he's mad about not being able to work out. The next time he annoys me, I'm going to tell him he's being a total shelter cat. Ha.

Liam and I stop at the park near my house for some snow cones. We're both exhausted from playing with all the dogs, but it's a good kind of exhaustion.

"I think I want to volunteer there on a regular basis," I say, taking a bite of my cherry snow cone.

"Totally." He slurps some melted ice from his snow cone cup and then reaches his plastic spoon over and steals a bite of mine. "This was the most gratifying day I've had in a while. Did you see how happy those dogs were? We totally made their day. I wish I could adopt all of them."

"Let's plan a day of the week where we're both free and we'll go volunteer."

He nods. "Say the word, and I'm there. Plus, we got a cardio workout in."

I roll my eyes. "Don't mention working out right now. You'll just remind me of my brother."

"Is he still being a jerk?"

I nod. "Oh yeah. You'd think his life is over if he's not at the gym. The other day he ordered a set of dumbbells off Amazon and had them delivered so he can work out his arms while he's sitting in the recliner."

Liam laughs. "I wish I had that much drive. Now that I'm not racing professionally anymore, I'm losing my six pack."

I lean against his shoulder while we sit on this park bench and watch two children fly a kite. "I still think you're extremely hot. Six pack or not."

8

LIAM

I have to wake up entirely too early on Monday morning because I've got a full day of job opportunities planned and I totally forgot about an essay that's due for one of my online classes. I fill my mom's coffee pot with dark roast and write until the sun rises. Once I'm fairly sure this essay will get me at least a B, I upload it and then get dressed with fifteen minutes to spare. We have a long drive today, and I can't wait to take Bella on this adventure.

She opens her front door looking exhausted and like she needs some of that coffee I drank earlier.

"Why so early?" she whines, tossing her head back with a groan.

"First of all, most careers will make you get up early and get to work by eight in the morning, so I'm actually doing you a favor," I say, poking her in the stomach. "You ready to go?"

She turns around to where her brother is watching us from his recliner in the living room. "You need anything before I leave?"

"Nah, I'm good," he says, not looking at me. I know I can't expect us to be friends, but a slight head nod of acknowledgment would be nice.

Bella steps onto her porch and closes the door behind her. "Do I look okay?"

"You always look way more than okay."

She rolls her eyes. "It's too early for your romantic compliments," she says, leaning up on her toes to kiss me. "I mean my clothes. Are they good for whatever you have planned today?"

I pretend to take a moment surveying her dark jeans and purple shirt. "We're going to the beach so…"

She puts her hands on her hips. "The beach in February? It's way too cold to swim."

I wiggle my eyebrows. "Good thing we're not swimming."

It's a three-hour drive to Galveston beach, which is off the gulf coast of Texas. It's not the prettiest beach ever, since the sand is often filled with dead seaweed and the water is sludge brown, but it's still a beach. I loved coming here as a kid because my dad would rent a luxury condo on the water and we'd spend all week in the sun and ocean, pretending to surf. But the other bad thing about Galveston beach is that the surf totally sucks. You're lucky if there's a wave big enough to even stand up on your surf board. We've got nothing on the west coast.

Now that Bella and I are dating, it feels wrong for her to sit way over on the passenger seat in my truck. "Hey," I say, reaching over and taking her hand. I tug on it. "Come closer."

She grins and slides across the bench seat, wrapping her hand around my arm while I drive. "That's better," I say. "You smell amazing."

"*You* smell amazing," she says.

"This is the best part of having a girlfriend," I say, kissing the top of her head while I focus on the road.

"Smelling me?" she teases.

I shake my head. "No, just all of it. Sitting next to you. Hanging out every day. Planning adventures. *And* smelling you," I add with a wink.

Long drives don't feel long when I'm with Bella. We listen to music and she snuggles against my shoulder and we stop off at the largest gas station I've ever seen and load up on snacks. Before I know it, we're in Galveston, parking on the seawall that overlooks the Gulf of Mexico.

I squeeze her leg. "You ready to try out your next career option?"

She glances out at the water. "Am I going to be a surfer?"

"Nope. You're going to save them."

It's cold outside but luckily, it's not too windy as we make our way down the concrete steps that lead to the beach. I didn't arrange this one ahead of time because I wasn't able to find any lifeguards online, so I'm just going to wing it. Hopefully it works.

We walk up to the first wooden lifeguard tower. There's a guy sitting in there, wearing a wetsuit and sunglasses.

"Hey there," I call out. "Could we talk to you about your job for a minute?"

I'm a little worried that he'll tell us to leave him alone, but instead he shrugs. "Sure. Come on up."

"You are very ambitious," Bella whispers as we walk up the stairs that lead to the tower.

I chuckle. "Hey, it's a job. Aquatics was on my potential career list. I thought we'd try something water-related."

The lifeguard's name is Jake and he tells us all about his job. He works for the city and it's a full-time gig since the beach is open year-round. He tells us there isn't much downtime even during the winter because people are always out here swimming even in the cold. We chat for a while, and then we let him get back to his job.

"So, what did you think?" I ask as we walk back to my truck.

Bella's upper lip curls. "Eh…"

"No worries. We still have two stops left."

Bella adjusts the radio, turning down the volume.

"What if I don't find anything? What if you take me to a hundred places and none of them inspire anything in me? What if I'm just some pathetic loser who will work at a fast food place my whole life?"

I frown. "First of all, you are not a pathetic loser. Secondly, I love fast food."

She rolls her eyes, and I smile. "Don't stress, babe. Just think of these trips as fun excursions. Maybe you'll end up loving one of these careers, or maybe you won't. You've got time to figure it out."

"I guess you're right," she says.

I know the next trip won't be career-worthy, but it seemed fun when I was looking up other stuff to do here in Galveston. We go to one of the historic and beautifully preserved mansions that were built back in the late 1890s. There are tours held here every hour, and Bella and I get in line for the next one.

"How is this a career?" she whispers as we wait on the wraparound Victorian porch.

"Tour guides, antique home restoration..." I say, looking around. Our tour guide appears, and she's dressed to the nines in a long flowy gown and bonnet that looks straight out of those Jane Austen movies my mom always watches late at night. "Costume design?"

Bella examines the woman's outfit. "That could be fun..."

Our tour begins, and there are five of us in the

group. Bella and I hang in the back, letting the three elderly woman who are with us stay closer to the tour guide since it looks like they could use the help hearing her. It's fun learning about how people lived over a hundred years ago. No central air conditioning, no electricity, but the homes were beautiful. I wonder if my dad would appreciate something like this, or if his architectural affections are only for the large and expensive designs.

An hour later, we're just in time for the third meeting I've arranged for her. We get back in my truck and drive down to the other side of town where my Aunt Riley works.

"Real estate," Bella says as we pull into the parking lot. "Nice."

"It seems fun," I tell her. "My aunt is excited to meet you."

"Ooooh," Bella says, clasping her hands together in front of her chest. "I get to meet one of your family members?"

"Yep. My mom's sister. Don't believe anything she tells you about my rebellious toddler years, okay?"

Aunt Riley greets us with smiles and freshly baked cookies. She's my mom's older sister by twelve years, and unlike my mom who frequently dyes her hair brown, Aunt Riley's hair is a pepper gray, pulled into a ponytail, that bounces as she hands me the tray of cookies.

"I'm so happy to meet you," she says, giving Bella a hug. "Here's your first lesson: freshly baked cookies will fill a house with the scent of home. Always have some ready when you're doing an open house."

"I can get behind working with cookies," Bella says.

Aunt Riley grins. "I just took pictures of a new house today. Come with me. I'll show you my office and how I post a new listing online."

"Sounds fun," Bella says. This is the most interested she's been all day. Maybe my final stop here in Galveston will be a good one.

Aunt Riley puts an arm around me. "Nephew, will you sit here and man the front desk? My assistant is out to lunch."

"Sure thing." I drop into the rolling chair that's behind the front desk and sit up straight, lacing my fingers together on top of the counter. "Do I look official?"

"You look very handsome," my aunt says with a sarcastic grin. "But not like you sell real estate."

I hang out up here while Bella and my aunt retreat to her office. Luckily, no one calls or comes into this small workplace, because I'm not sure what I'd do other than go back to my aunt and tell her someone was here. After about ten minutes, the door opens and I sit up, hoping I can look moderately professional as I greet this potential customer.

But the girl who walks in is wearing a black button up shirt with my aunt's logo on it.

"You must be the assistant?" I say, getting up from her chair.

"Yep. I'm Andrea." She takes off her sunglasses and her eyes widen. "Oh my God, you're Liam Mosely!" She drops her car keys and Starbucks cup on the counter and turns to me, all smiles. "I'm a huge fan."

Those are words I haven't heard in a few weeks, and honestly, I'd almost forgotten what it was like to be around fangirls.

"Oh… uh, thanks."

Her tongue darts out over her bottom lip. "So… what are you doing here? I've been telling Mrs. Riley to invite you over for ages. She always says you're busy traveling and stuff."

"Well, not anymore," I say, scratching my neck. I'm still not sure how to announce to people that I've quit the professional motocross scene. I guess I keep hoping that everyone will already know. "My traveling days are officially done."

Her eyes light up like I've just told her something special. "That's cool," she says, leaning a little closer. "So, you're in Houston full time now?"

"Yeah. Well, Roca Springs, actually."

"I don't know where that is," she says, smiling brightly. She reaches out and runs her fingers down my arm. "But I'd love for you to show me."

Whoa. Not good.

I can't believe I didn't realize this girl was flirting with me. Man, I'm off my game. There was a time in my life, not so long ago, that I already knew every girl who came around was interested in me. Funny how a few weeks with Bella makes me forget all about that.

I take a step backward. "It's a three hour drive away," I say, making extra sure to have no sign of flirting in my voice.

She is undeterred. Her eyelashes blink a few times as she gazes up at me, her lip slightly poked out. At first glance, you might not notice it, but I do. I've been flirted with enough times to notice that slight lip pout.

"I have a girlfriend," I blurt out. "She's actually back in my aunt's office learning about real estate."

Andrea's flirty demeanor doesn't change one bit. "She doesn't have to know anything," she whispers, reaching out and touching my arm again. She gives me a sultry look and then winks. "I'm very discrete."

I can't help myself. I burst out laughing. Covering my mouth with my fist, I shake my head. "Oh my God, no. I'm sorry but no. My girlfriend is amazing and—well, no. Frankly, I'm offended that you think I'm that type of guy."

Her expression turns to ice. "*Every* guy is that type of guy if the right offer comes along," she hisses.

"Oh well," she says, flipping her hair and walking behind the front desk to her chair. "Your loss."

There are some things I do miss about being a professional motocross racer. The money, for one. The factory bikes that were maintained by professional mechanics that ran like a dream. The cool free clothing by brands I love.

But this? Flirty girls who think I owe them something just because they want it?

I don't miss this at all.

9

BELLA

It's not even very late by the time we're driving back home, but I'm exhausted. I loved all of the career adventures that Liam took me on today. I don't think I could ever be a lifeguard, mostly because I'm not a great swimmer and I don't want to get skin cancer from being outside all day. The mansion we toured was so surreal and awe-inspiring that I make Liam promise me we'll go visit all five historic mansions in town and take the tours for all of them one day. But do I want to be a tour guide? Not really. Public speaking and I do not make a good pair.

The best trip of the day was to meet Liam's aunt. She was really nice and reminded me a lot of his mom. They're both sweet women who make you feel right at home. I'm not totally in love with the real estate agent career, but it's my favorite one so far.

She told me about how the classes you take to become licensed aren't that hard, and she even offered to hire me if I decide to pursue that path. The bad thing is that you only get paid when you sell a house. I don't want to live with the stress of not getting a paycheck if the market is down.

Despite how I had a great time at his aunt's office, Liam seems like he's in a bad mood when we leave. He turns up the radio and doesn't talk as we begin the three hour drive back home. I snuggle up next to him in the middle seat of his truck, laying my head on his shoulder. He wraps his arm around me as he drives, the cruise control on.

"You okay?" I ask him.

"Perfect," he says back. But I'm not sure I believe him. He's looking weird. Maybe he's just exhausted, too. We woke up really early and have spent the entire day doing stuff. Plus, he's had to drive the whole time. Maybe that's it.

"Are you tired?" I ask.

He shakes his head. "Nah."

"Then what's wrong?"

"Nothing, babe."

I get the sense he wants me to drop it, so I do. This is a first for us, an uncomfortable silence that I don't quite understand. It's not like we got in an argument or anything. So why is he acting weird?

I close my eyes, and when I open them again, we

are in Roca Springs. I sit up, yawning. "Holy crap. I slept the whole way home?"

Liam nods, his gaze on the road. "Yep."

I put a hand to my mouth. "I didn't drool on you, did I?"

"Nah. You sleep like an angel."

It's a sweet thing to say, but I can tell he's still not feeling exactly like himself. Something is bothering him, and it bothers me that he's not telling me about it. I guess this relationship won't be one hundred percent perfect, after all. Suddenly I'm filled with worries and apprehension. Is he having second thoughts about me? Am I boring him? What's going on?

His phone rings, and his mom's name shows up on the Bluetooth receiver on his truck's radio. He answers the call through his truck.

"Hey, mom," he calls out. "Bella is here so don't say anything that will embarrass me."

"Hi, Bella!" his mom says, her voice sounding all around us as it comes through the speakers. "How was your day in Galveston?"

"We had fun," I say, glancing at Liam, hoping his expression confirms my answer. He gives me a half smile.

"When will you be home?" she asks.

"Five minutes," Liam answers.

"Perfect! You'll be here in time for dinner. Bella, will you join us?"

"Sure," I say. Liam's mom makes the best food. I'll happily stay for dinner anytime. It's not until after the phone call is over that I remember how Liam is being kind of funny. I nudge him with my elbow. "I can go home if you want."

"What? No." He slows down and makes a right turn into his driveway. "I always want you around me."

I wish I could just let it go and not stress about this, but he's definitely being weird. He's trying to look normal, but I can tell something is bothering him. The moment he turns into his driveway, I am hit with the answer like a brick to the face. I feel so stupid for not realizing it sooner.

Liam is upset with me because he's done all this work and I haven't loved any of the career ideas he's found for me.

"Liam?" I say, turning toward him after I unbuckle my seatbelt.

He shuts off the engine and takes out the keys. "Yeah, babe?"

"I know why you're upset, and I'm sorry." My hands twist together in my lap.

His jaw flexes. "You have nothing to be sorry about."

I shake my head. "Yes, I do. You're trying so hard and here I am just being a brat who doesn't like anything. I'm so sorry, Liam." I look up and meet his concerned gaze. "I really am so grateful for all you've done. Seriously. And you've given me a lot to think about. I'm just…" I heave a sigh. "I'm just worthless, I guess. A total non-passionate non-talented person with zero career potential."

Liam looks at me for a long moment. And then he starts laughing.

"Liam!" I smack his arm playfully. "Don't laugh at me. I said I'm sorry and I mean it. I didn't mean to waste your time."

He takes my face in both of his hands. "Oh, babe. You are so sweet and perfect and—" He leans forward and kisses me. "You are *not* non-talented. And you haven't done anything wrong."

"Then why are you acting so weird?" I ask.

A shadow catches my attention and I see Matt, Liam's little six-year-old brother staring at us through the living room window, no doubt wondering when we'll come inside and play with him.

Liam notices Matt too and he waves at him. "It doesn't matter. I just got annoyed today, but it had nothing to do with you, I swear." He kisses me again. The shadow in the window disappears because Matt thinks kissing is gross. "Don't you worry about a thing."

"Are you sure?" I ask. "Because I feel really bad. You're trying so hard and I just don't know what to do with my life."

Liam's soft lips stretch into a smile. "Baby, I'm

not doing these career adventures as a way to force you to find something to do. I'm just doing it for fun. Because I love spending time with you."

I tilt my head. "Really? Because I feel bad."

He runs a hand through my hair. "You have nothing to feel bad about. You are the greatest thing to ever happen to me."

I throw my arms around him. "I'm not as cool as a six-figure racing contract," I mumble against his chest.

He chuckles and hugs me back. "No. You're much, *much* better."

LIAM

Spring Break weekend was probably the worst time for Bella and me to plan a day at the local motocross track. We haven't gone dirt bike riding together since last summer before I turned pro. It seemed like a good idea last night when we made the plans. I haven't been on my bike for fun in months. Riding with Team Loco was always work. You couldn't just have fun and putt around on the track, feeling the wind in your face. Nope. It was all training. All business. All work.

Last night while we were hanging out in my room, when I got the idea to take a day off from all this career research and go riding instead, neither one of us remembered that it was the start of spring break.

Now, as I drive into the track with Bella in the passenger seat, we both turn to look at each other.

"Spring freaking break," she says, palming her forehead. "I completely forgot."

"At least our spot is empty," I say, navigating through the crowded parking lot. Seems like every dirt-bike-owning person in the state decided to show up today. Roca Springs Motocross Park is fairly small, as far as dirt bike tracks go, and a good day might have twenty riders here.

Today it looks like there's a hundred.

I park next to the ancient oak tree that's right on the border of the property. It's off the main stretch of parking spaces, and it's so far away from the track that most people don't bother coming here. It's the place where I fell in love with Bella. I know I haven't told her yet, because we've only been officially dating for a few weeks and I don't want to be weird, but I love her. I love this girl. I know, without a single shred of doubt, that I do.

One day soon, when the time is right, I'll tell her.

After we park, I let down the tailgate and unload our bikes while Bella takes out our riding gear and folding lawn chairs. We have a routine, Bella and I, and it's really comforting. Most girls don't know crap about motocross, but my girl loves it as much as I do.

I put my dirt bike on the stand and run my hand down the worn seat cover. This old Yamaha brings back some good memories. It's a great bike and I've taken good care of it over the last couple of years, but it's got nothing compared to the factory ride I had for Team Loco. Their professional bikes cost at least thirty grand. I think I've put only about ten grand into my personal bike. But I love it even more because it's mine.

"Should I be jealous?" Bella says, giving me a flirty look as she shoves my helmet into my hands. "You're staring at your bike like it's a hot babe."

I laugh. "I was just thinking about how much I love this bike. Sure, it's not as fast as a factory Team Loco bike, but it's mine."

Bella leans closer to my bike and says, "Stop trying to steal my man or I'll cut your tires."

I gasp sarcastically. "How rude!"

She laughs and throws her arms around my neck. "This is fun. I miss being at the track with you."

"I missed it too. I can't wait to get out there and chase you around the dirt." We kiss, but I keep it quick or else my desire to make out will take over and we'll never get out on the track.

As soon as I steer my bike onto the track, following right behind Bella, I feel a sense of relief wash over me. This is where I was meant to be. This is how I should feel when I'm riding my dirt bike. Happy. Free. Alive. The last few weeks of racing professionally took all those good feelings away from me. It left me feeling like racing was a chore. Like dirt bikes were controlling my life and that it'd never be fun again. But now the pressure is off.

I kick it into third gear, and then fourth, and zoom over a double jump, staying right behind Bella. I could pass her, but I don't. She rides faster when I'm back here pushing her, and the view of her adorable backside makes it worth not going as fast as possible. I breathe in the spring air that's mixed with exhaust. It might not be good for my lungs, but it's good for my soul.

After a few laps, I pull off the track to get a drink. Bella stays out there, practicing her take offs at the starting line.

I only manage to take one sip of my Gatorade before someone approaches me. Make that two someones.

I turn around at the sound of the footsteps and see two girls about my age walking up. They're dressed in regular clothes, so they must not be here to ride.

"Hi, Liam," the brunette on the left says. "I'm Sarika. I'm a huge fan."

"I'm a bigger fan," the other girl says. She flips her hair over her shoulder and beams at me. "I'm Heather."

"Nice to meet you," I say, taking another sip of my drink in the hopes that I'll look bored enough for them to walk away. Maybe I'm a jerk, but I'm not technically famous anymore. I no longer ride professionally, and I don't feel like they're entitled to my time when I'm here as a regular person, not a celebrity.

"So why did you quit Team Loco?" Sarika says. "There are a lot of rumors going around."

"Don't believe the rumors." I wipe the sweat off my face with a hand towel and toss it back into the bed of my truck. "The reason I left is on my social media, and in about every interview I did on my last week with the team."

Heather rolls her eyes. "Yeah, we've seen the official watered-down answer," she says, taking a step closer. Her friend is right on her heels. Now they're basically crowding me up against the tailgate of my truck. "We want to know the real answer. Is it true you got that girl pregnant and she's threating you?"

I stare dead-eyed at her for a good five seconds. She doesn't take the hint and leave, even though I wish she would. "What did I just tell you about rumors?" I say.

I'm not under contract anymore, and therefore I'm under no obligation to be nice to people to say rude crap.

"We won't tell anyone," she says. "We're just really big fans and we don't want to see anyone try to damage your reputation."

"Plus, she's wondering if you're single," Sarika says. Her friend blushes and tries to look embarrassed, but I'm pretty sure it's all an act. They came over here hoping to what? Flirt with me? Win me over? Steal me from my girlfriend that is literally just across the track from us?

Speaking of… I really don't want Bella to come back here and see these girls bothering me. I don't want anything to happen that will ruin her day or make her question our relationship.

Instead of cursing them out like I really, really want to, I decide to be as nice as possible. Turning the other cheek and all that. "I'm very happy with my girlfriend. Anything you hear about me that doesn't come from my own mouth is a rumor and shouldn't be believed."

I stand up and put the cap back on my Gatorade. "Excuse me, I'm late for a meeting."

As I walk away, I try not to laugh at my own silly excuse. Late for a meeting? With who? We're at a dirt bike track! But it was the first thing that came out of my mouth, and I'm desperate to put as much space between me and those awful girls before Bella gets off the track.

So, I keep walking, straight toward the office building at the entrance to the track. They don't follow me, luckily, but I'm stopped by a few people along the way. Most of them want to say hello or tell me that they're "big fans" of my racing career. One person asks why I quit Team Loco and I tell them to look online.

Eventually, I make it to the building in one piece, with no annoying fans trying to follow me inside. The building is mostly empty, with only the employee who sits behind the front counter here. She signs in people and takes their money, but mostly she just sits here on her phone. There's a TV in the corner of the room playing a loop of motocross DVDs.

"Hi," she says, smiling at me. She's always been friendly and never oversteps the bounds of politeness by asking some rude invasive question. I think she's the owner's daughter. "Can I help you with anything?"

I sigh and place my hands on the front counter. "No," I admit. "I just lied and said I needed to come here for a meeting just so I could avoid these annoying fans who kept asking rude stuff."

"Oh," she says, eyes widening. "That's awful. I'm sorry."

"Rude stuff?" a man says from the other room. Soon, the track owner emerges from his office which is behind the front counter. He's about fifty years old, I guess, and he's always been extremely nice to me. "Who was it? I'll have them escorted off the property."

I shrug. "Eh, it's no big deal. Just annoying."

"It can be hard transitioning back into the real world after being pro," he says.

"You were pro?" I ask. Mentally, I run his name

through all the old pros I know and I can't remember him.

"Barely," he says with a nod. "Back in the nineties. I made it on a Kawasaki professional team for one year. I never did too great, and they ended up dropping me from the team. But when I came back home, I was a celebrity in my local motocross community."

"He acts humble," his daughter says with a roll of her eyes. "But he'll gladly talk about his days of fame forever if you let him."

He waves off his daughter's playful insult. "Oh, shush. I'm just commiserating with the boy. I'm glad to have you back, though, Liam. You're a good kid and you bring a lot of business to the track."

I laugh. "How did you get over all the attention?"

"It'll fizzle out after a while," he says, leaning on the counter. He gazes off at the wall, his thoughts clearly back in another time. "It was fun while it lasted, though. Every now and then one of the old-timers will come here and recognize my name and we'll get to talking. It's fun being remembered. You hate it now, but you might like it later on."

"Did you own the track before or after you went pro?" I ask.

"Way after," he says. "I did a bit of time as a manager at a hardware store and that just wasn't for me. Then this land went up for sale and since it floods a lot, no one could build a house on it. So it was dirt cheap. And I thought, hey what better use for cheap dirt than a dirt bike track?"

His daughter snorts at his joke.

"That's cool," I say. "It seems to have worked out for you."

"Oh yeah, best decision I ever made. You thinking of owning your own track one day?"

I bite down on my bottom lip. "Honestly, that never occurred to me until now."

"You should do it, son. Not anywhere close to here because you'll steal all my business—" he snorts out a laugh. "But running a track is pure joy. I promise. You get to be involved with the best sport in the world, and you get paid to do it."

The gears in my mind start turning. I know Bella has been worried about what she'll do with her life, but I've kind of been avoiding my future for now.

"That's definitely worth thinking about," I say. "Not sure there's any cheap land to turn into a track now, though."

"You should talk to old man Bailey," he says, pointing a finger at me. "I hear that old geezer is about to retire soon. He's wanting to sell the track."

"Really?" Mr. Bailey owns Oakcreek Motocross, which is a pretty well-known track about three hours from here. I used to love riding there when I was a kid.

"Ooh, that would be cool," his daughter says. "We

could partner up Roca Springs and Oakcreek for a series race!"

"It's worth a shot," he says. "Trust me, owning your own track is a dream. Best job ever."

"Thanks," I tell him, even though I'm sure that kind of thing costs way too much money. "I think I might look into it."

11

BELLA

*L*ife is starting to feel normal now. Being a girlfriend and having an amazing relationship with Liam is now just my regular life. I can honestly say I've never been so happy in all of my life. My college classes are easy, my riding skills are constantly getting better, and making out with Liam every day is definitely a perk of being me. We haven't taken things much further than making out yet. Sometimes I really want to, but other times I like taking things slowly. It kind of feels like once we've experienced all the "firsts" with each other, it won't be as special anymore.

Plus, I keep reminding myself that even though I've basically been in love with him for ten months, we've only been dating for less than two.

It's Thursday night and Liam is on his way over

with take out Chinese food. We're going to watch some superhero movie tonight at my place.

Brent still isn't able to walk on his broken leg yet, but he's no longer stuck on the recliner. He's moved back to his bedroom, where he sulks quietly alone in there. I try to remember to visit him every few hours so he doesn't get bored, but he's not really much fun to be around. The insurance company totaled his truck and he got a big check from them to buy a new one. All he ever talks about now is how he can't wait to go car shopping once he can walk again. He starts physical therapy soon. I hope that once he's back on his feet (literally and metaphorically) he'll stop being so gloomy and annoying.

"Your boyfriend is here," Brent calls out from his room. I'm in the living room which has a window that looks out into the front yard just like Brent's bedroom does. So he knows I can see Liam arrive just as well as he can. I think he just likes to point it out to be annoying.

I ignore him and answer the door.

"They gave us free cookies," Liam says, wiggling his eyebrows excitedly as he holds up the take-out food. "The owner said I'm her best customer because I order there twice a week."

"You keep eating junk like that and you'll get fat," Brent calls out from his bedroom.

"Fat but happy," Liam calls back.

This is how they are now. My brother and

boyfriend, not exactly friends, but not exactly enemies. It's not perfect, but I'll take it.

After we eat, I snuggle up against Liam on the couch. He's highly into the superhero movie, but I find them kind of boring. There's too many of them out there now, and I get lost in the overlapping storylines. The only thing these superhero movies are good for in my opinion, is the sexy eye candy actors, and now that I'm dating Liam, who is sexier than all of them combined, I don't really care.

I lean against Liam's chest and play on my phone for most of the movie. His fingers absentmindedly play with my hair while he watches the TV. I love this so much. Just hanging out with him. Life is good.

Somehow, in my bored internet browsing, I end up on the Facebook page for Oakcreek Motocross. I notice they're having a women's only race day, hosted by this Texas racer named Morgan who is locally famous and totally awesome. There will be ten different races, one for each age group and bike size, and the whole thing goes to support a battered women's shelter.

I sit up on the couch. "Liam! I want to race this weekend!"

He pauses the TV. "I didn't think there was a race this weekend?"

"It's at Oakcreek," I say, showing him my phone.

"All the money goes to a women's charity and it'll be all girls racing. This will be so cool."

Oakcreek is a long drive away, and we'd have to leave at four in the morning to get there, but I'm surprised when he eagerly agrees. "That sounds amazing," he says. "Let's do it."

"Really?" I squeal. I've never ridden on that track, and I'm a little scared, but I think it'll be fun. Plus, it'll be all girls racing. Freaking girl power to the max.

He grins. "I've actually been wanting to go there, so this is good timing."

"You should wear a disguise, so no one notices you," I say, cupping his face in my hands. "A track full of girls means a track full of girls who will all want to flirt with you."

He wraps his arm around me and hoists me up onto his lap in one swift, strong motion that totally turns me on. "Too bad for them. I've already found the girl of my dreams."

OAKCREEK MOTOCROSS PARK IS IN THE TEXAS HILL country, where the land is all sloped, with rolling hills that make the natural terrain perfect for a motocross track. Unlike at home, our land is mostly flat and all the jumps have to be man-made, here they've taken the natural hills and turned them into jumps. There are large pine trees all over the place, and the whole track is beautiful. It's like nature and motocross combined into one.

I'm in awe as we walk around the facility. Someone has decorated the track with hot pink plastic flags instead of the multicolored ones that are usually put up for races. It's kind of stereotypical to decorate the track in all pink to celebrate women, but whatever. It's the spirit of the race that makes me happy. Tons of women from all over the state have showed up today in support of the race.

I decide to sign up for the 250f novice class, since I'm not quite a beginner, but not advanced enough to put myself in the "expert" class.

Liam took my advice with the whole disguise thing… he's wearing a plain T-shirt instead of one of the hundreds of dirt bike shirts he owns, and a Houston Astros baseball cap pulled low over his eyes, which are covered with sunglasses. If he's not all decked out in dirt bike brands, maybe people won't notice him. So far, it seems to be working.

The first hour before the races start is for practice. Everyone gets to ride around and get a feel for the track. I'm at a disadvantage because I've never been on this track before, and after a few slow laps, I'm feeling more than a little nervous. This isn't the same track as my home track. It's harder, and different, and a little challenging.

By the time I pull off the track, I'm almost in

tears. Maybe I should have signed up for the beginner level race after all.

I need to see my boyfriend and have him tell me all those sweet words he's so good at. My vision is blurred with tears as I slowly ride back to his truck. When I get there, I see him surrounded by girls. I have to bite back more tears. I wanted him to myself. I didn't want to share him today.

I park my bike and pull off my helmet.

"Hey babe," Liam calls out.

I nod at him in reply. Then I pull off my helmet. I'm very much aware of the fact that I'm sweaty and miserable and have helmet hair and the four girls who are standing next to my boyfriend are wearing cute outfits, nice makeup, and aren't covered in sweat. Liam breaks away from them and walks over to me. "How was the track?"

Before I can answer, the girls have all turned their attention to me.

"What's your name?" one says.

"Bella," I say quickly, looking back at Liam. "The track was okay. It's kind of hard," I admit.

We're clearly in our own conversation right now but Liam's fans aren't having any of it. The girl who asked for my name takes a step closer. She's not even trying to hide her jealous glare and judgmental assessment of what I look like. "So you're the girl who made Liam quit?"

"I'm sorry, who are you?" I say in the best rude

voice I can muster. Normally I might be better at it, but I'm still holding off tears from how disappointing my practice ride was.

"I'm a concerned fan," she says, smiling that evil girl smile that my gender saves just for other women. "Liam was a favorite member of Team Loco and none of us appreciate you making him quit."

My mouth falls open. I am all out of sarcastic replies to spit back at them.

"That's enough," Liam says, stepping between me and them, like a human shield. "You're being extremely rude, so I'm asking you to leave. If you talk to my girlfriend again, I'll be telling park security about you."

"Ugh, she made you a jerk too," the girl says. But she and her friends turn and leave without saying anything else. At least not anything loud enough for me to hear.

I burst into tears.

"Baby," Liam says, rushing up to me. He holds my face in his hands, pressing his forehead to mine. He doesn't even seem to care that I'm sweaty and gross. "Baby don't cry. Forget about them. They're the ones with a problem, not us."

I shake my head and try to take a breath, but it comes out all ragged. "It's not them... It's—well it's kind of them," I admit. "But it's also me. This track is hard. I mean, it's beautiful and I love it but there's no way I'll win the race tonight. Not even close. I need more practice."

"Baby," Liam says softly, his lips just inches from mine. "Take a deep breath."

I do as he says. He kisses my forehead, and then wraps his arms around me. We sway a little bit as if he were slow dancing, and it's like he's trying to hug the fears out of me. I relax into him, breathing slowly.

"This is just a fun race. For fun. For charity. Try not to let it stress you out."

"Easier said than done," I mumble against his chest.

He chuckles and continues to hold me, swaying ever so softly. I feel so safe and perfect in his arms. I almost wish we never had to let go. "All these people are judging you and judging me," I say. "If I get last place, they're going to know you're dating a loser."

"It only takes one look at you to realize I'm dating someone way out of my league," Liam says. "Anyone who thinks otherwise can go suck a lemon."

"You are completely wrong, but I don't feel like arguing with you right now," I say, smiling up at him.

"Smart move," he says, kissing me. "Because that's an argument you'd lose.

I roll my eyes.

He just grins and kisses me again.

12

LIAM

As Bella gets ready to go to the starting line for her race, I'm remembering conversations from my days on Team Loco. Keanna Adams had told me all about how hard it can be to be the girlfriend or wife of a racer. Fans can be extremely rude to girlfriends, and it's a hard thing to deal with. Back then, I was single, so I didn't put much thought into it. But now I see exactly what she meant. I hate this, so much.

I hate seeing how nervous Bella is before the race. I hate the way those girls looked at her earlier. They don't like her just because she's my girlfriend. You know what? I'm glad I quit racing. I'm going to live my life for me now, without the fame or the money that comes from being a professional racer. It's just not worth it. Soon, I'll be old news and people won't care about me anymore. I'll fade away from people's minds, getting replaced with new professional racers they can love and adore. Then Bella and I can have a real relationship.

"You ready?" I ask her as she pulls on her helmet and straddles her bike.

Her shoulders rise and fall with a deep breath. She nods once, her helmet bobbing. "As ready as I'll ever be."

I reach for her gloved hand and give her a squeeze. "You'll be great. Tell your nerves to piss off."

She laughs. "I'll try."

I jog alongside her as she rides up to the starting line. There are at least twenty other girls racing with her, making this a lot bigger of a race than she's used to. I blow her a kiss and then jog over to the bleachers so I can get a good view of the race. This track is large and sprawling, taking up several acres of sloping land, so I won't be able to see the entire track from any one viewpoint.

I walk up to the top of the bleachers, where I can see as much of the track as possible. A few people seem to recognize me from the bleachers, but I ignore them. I try to look uninterested and hope that no one talks to me. My sunglasses shield my eyes, and my hat does a pretty good job of keeping most of my face hidden. Maybe I should dye my hair and grow it out long so I can blend in even better. I'm sick of being recognized.

I sit on the bleacher seat and watch the starting

line. Bella got a good spot, right in the middle of the gate. If she gets a good holeshot, she'll be able to pull out ahead of most of the other riders. While I'm watching the track, I can tell someone is looking at me. Knowing my eyes can't be tracked through my dark sunglasses, I glance down and see a kid, probably only about seven years old, watching me.

I nod at him. He jumps, then turns back around.

On the track, the gate drops, and the racers take off. I watch intently as Bella pulls out in the lead, one of the fastest riders by far. I let out a whoop of pride as I see her become the first person to speed around the first turn. Then the track dips down below the tree line and I lose sight of her. But she was in first place. I'm so proud. Hopefully her nerves will wear off now that she's killing it out there. I always stopped being nervous shortly after the races started. It's before the gate drops that all your insecurities and fears buckle up inside you. But once you're riding, it all just eases up and you can focus.

"Excuse me," a man says as he stomps up the metal bleacher stairs. "You're Liam Mosely, right?"

"Uh, yeah," I say. I can't believe I almost lied, but there it is. On the tip of my tongue, I almost said *nope, not me. You've got the wrong guy.* But my face has literally been printed on T-shirts, so I'd be kind of stupid to deny it.

"I'm a big fan, big fan," the large man says as he shakes my hand. "You're a great rider."

"Thanks, man."

I finally get my hand back from his overly boisterous handshake and I spot Bella on the track. She's still in first place. A few seconds later, I lose sight of her behind a hill.

"It's cool that you're out here supporting the race," the man says.

"Yeah, I'm actually supporting my girlfriend," I say, not looking at him because I'm trying to find her on the track. "She's out there racing right now."

"Oh, right on. Very cool," he says. "I run the hot dog stand down at the food area. You come on by later and get some food on the house, okay? Your girlfriend too."

I look over at him and give him a grateful smile. He's just being nice and not being an annoying fan, so I shouldn't be so dismissive of him. "Thanks. I appreciate it."

He walks back down to where his family is sitting, and I pray that no one else recognizes me, at least not right now. I'm trying to focus on my girlfriend. When I find her again, she's in second place. Someone on a bike I've never seen before has passed her. That sucks, but second place out of all these people isn't too bad. Only four more laps to go. Maybe she'll be able to get back into first place.

I'm so focused on watching Bella race that I don't realize another person has approached me until she speaks. "Hello, Liam."

"I'm busy," I say, not taking my eyes off the track. Bella is so close to passing the person in front of her. She might actually win this. "I can't talk now."

"Too busy to talk to me?" The voice is annoyingly sweet, and it makes the hairs on the back of my neck stand up. I don't know how I know this voice, but I do. It's familiar.

I look over and almost don't recognize her at first. Her hair is longer, her makeup isn't as bold and smoky as it used to be. She's taller, and more mature. But it's the same girl.

Samantha.

"Long time no see," she says, reaching out to hug me.

I flinch away and she lowers her hands. "Fine," she says with a mock pout. "Don't hug me."

"I am not in the mood to deal with you." I look back at the track, hoping she'll leave. But she doesn't leave, and I can't concentrate anyway. All the bikes out on the track are just blurry figures, moving too fast for my addled brain to focus on.

"Aw, Liam, don't be mean," Samantha says. She slides closer to me on the bench. "We used to be friends."

"We were never friends."

"You're right," she says with a little carefree laugh. "We were more than friends." I hate how she gets to sit here, laughing and having fun, having no idea how much she's messed things up for me.

"You should go," I tell her. "I don't want to talk to you. I don't want to see you."

"Wow," she says, putting a hand to her chest. "Why? I thought we had fun."

"We didn't. And you almost ruined a really good thing for me, Samantha. I haven't seen you in years and yet you've still somehow managed to make my life harder. So just go. You're the last person I want to see right now."

"Wait… what are you talking about?"

I want to ignore her, but she seems genuinely confused, and maybe even a little hurt at how I'm treating her. I realize that what I did in my past was back when I was a stupid kid, and she was a stupid kid too. Maybe she's a nice person now, someone who isn't exactly worthy of my hatred.

"I'm sorry," I say, glancing at her quickly before looking back at the track. "I don't mean to be rude, but the last time I saw you, you ruined my friendship with Brent. Now I'm dating his sister and he totally hates me because of what you did."

"Brent?" She crinkles her nose. "Brent who? Oh! Castro?" She laughs. "Oh man, how is he? I forgot about him."

"How could you forget about someone you dated for years?"

She shrugs. "We weren't, like, serious or anything."

I give her a look.

"What?" she says defensively.

"He seemed to think you were exclusive. He liked you a lot. And now he hates me because of what we did."

"I'm sorry," she says with a shrug. "Tell him to get over it. Me and Brent were not exclusive in my mind… I must have made out with, like, every motocross guy my age back then. And even some who were way too old for me." She sighs and shakes her head. "I'm extremely embarrassed by my behavior, by the way. I'm not like that anymore, I swear."

I don't even know what to say to that. This girl is sitting here next to me acting like what happened a few years ago was so meaningless it wasn't even worth the memory. And yet, over here in my life, what we did has affected me so very much. It made my girlfriend's brother hate me. It made my girlfriend not trust me when we first met. It made me feel like an awful person for what I did.

But mostly, I'm just feeling a little sad for Brent. Every day since he caught me kissing his girlfriend has been spent in this bitter mood. He's never gotten over Samantha, and everyone knows it. And yet, ironically, this whole time, Samantha probably hasn't thought about him once.

13

BELLA

This raw energy takes over me when I'm on the race track. I'm not normally a competitive person in any other subject in the world, but with motocross, it's different. It's like this sheer willpower to win the race takes over my body and pushes me to ride faster and harder than normal. I'm doing it, too. I'm fast. Faster than I was in practice. Faster than I normally am at my home track. I'm in second place, and I want this so badly. My fingers ache from gripping the handlebars so hard.

I spin around a wide sweeping turn and then launch my bike over a jump. I am right. On. Her. Heels.

So close to passing her up.

But then the checkered flag flies and the race is over. Second place.

Ah well. That was still fun.

The adrenaline wears off the second I pull off the track and head back toward Liam's truck. My entire body aches as my muscles start to relax. I didn't realize how tuned in to the race I was until now, when it's over.

I don't see Liam waiting for me at the finish line like he normally does at our home track races. This is a much bigger track though, so he's probably waiting for me at his truck.

But he's not there either. I park my bike and then pull off my helmet, my chest heaving with heavy breaths. I'm in pretty good shape ever since I spent the summer practicing every day, but I feel exhausted right now. Like I just ran a marathon.

I climb up into Liam's truck bed and grab some water from the ice chest back here. I down half the bottle before I finally see him, walking up to the truck. He waves at me.

"Took you long enough," I say, tossing him a playful grin.

"I was on the bleachers. This is a huge freaking track."

I laugh and toss him a water bottle.

"You did amazing," he says, throwing his arm around my shoulders while we sit on his tailgate. "Second place, yeah? You were fantastic."

"What do you mean, yeah?" I say, elbowing him.

"You were watching me, right? You should know what place I got."

He hesitates. Takes a deep breath. "I was watching, but I got distracted."

"Annoying fangirls?" I say, trying not to let it bother me. Everywhere we go, Liam is surrounded by annoying fangirls. It is what it is.

"Not exactly." He chugs some of his water and then tosses the empty bottle into the bed of his truck.

Anxiety settles over my bones, making me tense up again. Something is clearly bothering him, and I'm not exactly sure I want to know what it is. But I also can't let it go. "What does that mean?"

He shrugs. "I just had a weird experience."

I give him a look to continue.

"Samantha is here."

I choke on my water.

Coughing, I take a deep breath and look at him. "What did she do?"

"She apologized, for one," he says, scratching the back of her neck. "It was weird. She acted like she didn't even care about your brother... like they weren't in a serious relationship or anything."

I snort. "Yeah, right! He was head over heels for that cheater."

"I guess she didn't feel the same way."

"Ugh," I say, curling my lip. "Let us never speak of her again. I don't want my day to be ruined."

Liam's gaze drifts off to somewhere behind me. "Oh, babe, I really wish I could make that promise."

An uneasy feeling falls over me as I slowly turn around. There she is, tall and as beautiful as I remember her, walking right in front of us. She doesn't see us, luckily, but it's hard to miss her. I remember her so very well. She was always with my brother. She was always so cool. I wanted to be just like her. And now, I can't stand the sight of her for two reasons.

She broke my brother's heart.

My boyfriend has made out with her.

The uneasy feeling in my stomach turns to anger. I know I shouldn't be jealous, but I am. She's made out with my boyfriend. Her stupid lips were on his stupid lips. I know I didn't know him back then and I know it shouldn't matter, but it does. I'm only human, filled with all these pathetic human emotions.

"Whatever you're thinking, don't," Liam says softly, squeezing his arm around my shoulders. "That's in the past. You're my present. And you're my future."

I force a smile and look up at him. "I know. But I still wish she wasn't here. It kind of ruins my awesome day."

"Think of it as a slight annoyance," he says. "Not a total day ruiner."

I grin. "I guess you're right."

He pops an invisible collar on his T-shirt. "Psh, I'm always right."

I punch him in the arm. "Don't go getting all cocky, Mr. Mosely."

Liam's fingers are quick, and soon he's tickling me and I'm unable to wriggle out of his grasp.

"Not fair!" I call out, laughing even though I don't want to. Being tickled is weird like that. You hate it, but you laugh anyway.

Liam stops tickling my sides, but his hands stay where they are, wrapping around my hips and pulling me in for a kiss.

"I smell like sweat," I say, pulling away.

"Why on earth would I care about that?" he says, kissing me. He tastes like lemon lime Gatorade, and I bet I taste the same way. I get lost in his arms for a few seconds. The loud rumble of dirt bikes on the track becomes just background noise to the main show, which is Liam's lips on mine. That's all I care about right now.

Then I hear, "Wow. Maybe you two need a room!"

I jump back as if I've been electrocuted. Samantha is here, having appeared out of thin air. I don't know when she saw us, but the last time I saw her, she was walking away from us.

"Looks like someone needs to mind their own business," Liam says. He flashes her a wry smile, the kind that is all fake niceness and one hundred percent snark.

She doesn't seem fazed one bit. "Hi, there. You're Bella, right?"

"Who are you?" I say, trying to do my best impression of not-giving-a-crap.

"It's me," she says with a big Texas-sized smile. "Samantha! I haven't seen you since you were a little kid!"

I'm only a few years younger than she is, but whatever. I can still remember how cool I used to think she was, and how badly I wanted to be her friend. Now that very thought feels repulsive.

"Oh, okay," I say, pretending like I only just now figured out who she was. I reach for my phone from the tailgate and unlock the screen, casually checking my messages instead of looking at her. "I think I remember you. Aren't you that girl who cheated on my brother?"

She actually looks a little upset, but only for a split second before she shrugs the thought away and replaces it with a sweet smile. "I didn't cheat on him. We weren't exclusive."

"Really? Because my brother thought you were exclusive… how weird is that?"

"Well, you know Brent," she says, waving her hand. "Always making more of an issue out of something than it is."

"Right… yeah, that sounds like Brent." I feel dirty

talking bad about my brother, but I do it anyway. "I remember he was so upset when you cheated on him that one time."

"One time?" She laughs. "If he thinks what me and Liam did was cheating, then he'd be pissed if he knew about the other guys."

I feel so, so, gross, but I lean forward and look intrigued instead. "Oooh, do tell! Any hot guys?"

Liam looks positively betrayed, but he doesn't say anything. I can feel his gaze burning into me though, but I just smile up at Samantha.

"You remember Jake Weston?" She says, in full on girl-gushing mode.

I nod.

"Him, and Brian... oh, what was his last name? That hot guy who rode the Kawasaki?"

"Oh, yeah, I remember him," I say. "He was one of Brent's friends, too."

"Oh yeah, they all hung out together." She reaches out for my hand and instead of repulsively jumping away, I let her take it. "Girl, there's no weird feelings now, okay? It's totally cool that you're dating Liam. He's off limits, I promise."

"Thanks, girl," I say, using her same tone of voice. "I really appreciate it. Hey, while we're on the subject, did Liam come on to you that day or did you flirt with him first?"

"That was a long time ago," she says, waving away my question. "He's all yours now, I promise."

"No, that's cool. I was just wondering if he had as much swagger back then as he does now?"

I can sense Liam's jaw tighten next to me. He's looking at me like I've just ripped out his heart and tossed it on the ground. I glance at him and smile, hoping he can read my mind, but the hurt expression on his face tells me he can't.

"Nah, he wasn't very suave," she says with a giggle that makes my skin crawl. "I had to work hard to get his attention. But good on you, girl. You seem to have won him over."

I beam up at her, my fake smile shining at its full wattage. "Thanks, girlie! I'm pretty proud of myself, too."

"Well, see you later!" She turns and walks away.

I exhale. Liam folds his hands over his chest.

"What was that for, Bella? You don't believe me? You just had to rub it in that I made a one-time mistake?"

"Babe…" I say, holding out my hand. "Please don't be mad. I'm sorry but… I had to do that."

His nostrils flare. "Why? She's old news. She's nothing to me."

I shake my head. "Of course. I know that. This isn't about you."

"Then what is it about?"

I hold up my phone and press play. The audio recording I sneakily took just a few minutes ago is loud and clear. Samantha's voice goes on and on, repeating how she happily cheated on my brother.

Liam's eyes widen. "I thought of a way to make Brent realize that he should hate *her*, not you. And the only way to get her to say what I need my brother to hear was to ask her."

14

LIAM

After that weirdness with Samantha earlier today, the rest of our day went really well. Bella won her second race, for an overall finish of first place. She got to bring home her first ever winning trophy, and because of the women-only race, the trophy is bright pink and sparkly. Even I have to admit it looks pretty cool. Bella is all smiles on the long drive home. She keeps glancing into the backseat where her trophy is laying on its side because it's too tall to stand up back there. She grins and then looks back at me.

"I'm glad we went today."

"Me too," I say. I haven't been to Oakcreek in years and I really wanted to see what it was like now. I can't stop thinking about the idea of buying the track one day – or any track—and running it. It could be a lot of fun. I don't know what Bella would think about it, though. I wanted to bring it up after the races, but then all that weirdness happened with Samantha, and I just put it out of my mind. I'll tell her about the idea of buying the track when we're not still breathing in the awkwardness of that talk with Samantha. I'm glad Bella did what she thought would help her brother, but I wish the whole talk hadn't happened.

I felt awful seeing Bella hear Samantha say those things. I don't want her feelings hurt. I don't want her to think in any way that I ever liked Samantha or cared about her beyond one stupid kiss.

I try really hard to put it all out of my mind while we drive. I just want to enjoy this time with my girl-friend and not think about the past.

We grab some dinner at a taco place on the way home and everything is going fine. The tacos are so good I almost totally forget about the Samantha thing.

And then when I drive up to Bella's house, she takes off her seatbelt and says, "Okay let me do all of the talking."

"Wait, what talking?" I put the truck in park and cut the engine. I still need to unload her dirt bike and put it in her garage, but then I figured I'd just go home since it's been a long day.

"With Brent," Bella says. "I'll do all the talking, and you just hang out next to me."

"You're going to tell him *now*?"

"Of course." She nods. "How else will I get him to forgive you and move on? It needs to happen now."

"Just wait until I go home," I say.

"No, Liam." Bella's expression is asking me, not exactly telling me that I should stay. "I want you here," she says softly. "This is about you. It's about you and me and Brent. I want us all here when I settle this once and for all."

Whelp. I can't say no to her.

My nerves are on fire as we walk into her house. "Brent?" she calls out, but he's sitting on the recliner again in the living room.

"Yeah?" he says, not even looking up from his show on TV.

"Can you pause that?"

Bella glances at me and I follow her to the couch. I'm really, really, not prepared for the amount of awkwardness that's about to happen, but I guess it's going to happen no matter what. When Bella is determined, she gets something done.

Brent looks at us suspiciously, like he's about to be thrown into an intervention or something. And, I guess that's pretty much what this is.

"Tell me the reasons you hate Liam," she says.

Brent rolls his eyes. "No, I'm serious," Bella goes on, glancing at me quickly. "Tell me why you don't like him."

"He made out with my girlfriend."

"Any other reason?" she asks.

He glares at me. "I guess not."

"Great," Bella says. She grins.

Brent and I are both making looks that are the exact opposite of a grin. Bella is undeterred.

"We were at the races today and we ran into Samantha," Bella says.

Brent blanches.

"I need you to listen to this." She holds out her phone and presses play.

Samantha's voice is clear, and it takes over the entire room. I'm grateful that their mom isn't home right now because the only thing more awkward would be if she was in the room listening, too.

Brent's expression turns stone cold, his jaw tight, as he listens to the conversation. When it's over, Bella puts her phone down and looks at her brother.

"You're a smart guy, Brent. You've got a four point oh GPA, so I know you're smart. You know what this means, right?"

His eyes meet mine and I try not to flinch or back away. "It means I should forgive your boyfriend? Is that what you're getting at?"

"Yeah, actually."

Brent swallows. "It means my girlfriend was cheating on me with a lot more people than him."

I can sense his heartbreak, feel it cracking right through his heart again as he relives all that pain he's been through over the years. He hasn't dated since Samantha. This has to be hard on him. Now that I'm an amazing relationship myself, I can't even fathom what I would feel if I walked in on Bella cheating on me with some other guy. I would hate the guy, for sure. I would be completely devastated.

"I'm sorry, Brent," Bella says. "I really am, but I had to show you. I couldn't just keep this from you."

He shakes his head. "No, I agree. Thanks. I needed to hear it. Now maybe I can get over her for good."

Bella smiles. "Does this mean you're okay with me and Liam dating?"

He looks at me, and then at his sister. "Yeah, I guess."

"Does this mean you'll stop hating him so much?"

"I don't hate him," Brent says. "He was there for me when I got in that wreck. He could have driven away, but he didn't. You're a good dude, man."

I give him a slight nod of appreciation. He holds out his fist toward me, the ultimate gesture of guy friendship. I reach out and bump my fist to his.

"Yay!" Bella says, bouncing on her seat. "My brother and boyfriend are friends at last."

Brent snorts. "Make sure you invite me to our best friends slumber party, man."

I laugh and Bella rolls her eyes. "You don't have to be sarcastic."

It feels good to know that the air has been cleared between Brent and me. That I've been forgiven. That we can move on. An old chapter in my life has been closed and a new one can begin, fresh and untainted.

Bella stands up and takes my hand. "Let's go find a place for my amazing new trophy."

I carry the pink sparkly thing into her bedroom and look around, genuinely trying to find a place for it. The door closes behind me. I turn around and see Bella looking at me with those alluring eyes of hers. She takes the trophy from my hand and places it on the floor.

"I don't really care about the trophy," she says, sliding her arms up my chest.

"Ahh," I say, grabbing onto her waist. "You're sneaky."

"Well, I'm not about to tell my brother to excuse us so we can go make out," she says, her voice slightly above a whisper. She grins up at me and I scoop her into my arms, wrapping her legs around my waist.

I lean forward and our lips touch, the kiss soft and eager all at once. With Bella in my arms, I walk her over to her bed and lay her down softly. She doesn't let go of me, so I come with her, tumbling onto the bed in a mess of arms and legs and kisses.

She smiles up at me, then closes her eyes. I go in for another kiss, reveling in the feel of her lips on mine. The softness of her tongue as it grazes across mine, sending a shiver down my spine.

I drink her in, every inch of her, and I'm so

grateful that she's mine. My hands slide down her arm, and up her hip, over her clothes. While we make out, I slowly inch my fingers up under the bottom of her shirt. My heart is pounding at the closeness of our bodies, the way her hands move through my hair, tugging me closer and deepening our kisses.

My hand slides up her side, and I feel her skin prickle with goosebumps beneath my fingertips. I lean over and kiss her cheek, then her neck, then her collarbone. Her breathing is ragged, but blissful, against my neck.

I reach for her hip again and squeeze her close to me, our bodies moving slowly together, entranced by each other.

When my eyes blink open, I see her staring at me, her face just inches away from mine. I kiss her softly and then smile. "What are you thinking?"

She shrugs and runs her finger down my arm. "I'm thinking that you never push me to do anything more than just make out."

"Is that a good thing, or a bad thing?"

Her smile is so seductive it makes my toes curl. "It's a good thing. Most guys try their hardest to push a girl further than she wants to go."

"I'm not most guys," I whisper, leaning in to kiss her neck. She gasps and then snuggles against me.

"Don't I know it. I'm one of the lucky ones. I somehow managed to snag a guy as amazing as you."

I want to say it. I want to say it so, so, badly. But would she think I'm only saying those words because we're in the heat of the moment?

When I tell her I love her I don't want there to be any doubt in her mind about my feelings for her. So I hold back. I lock the words up in my heart and replace them with more kisses.

One day soon I'll tell her.

15

BELLA

*L*iam isn't letting me off the job search hook for spring break. Once more, we wake up early and drive down to Houston, where he's arranged a meeting with one of his dad's accountants. I feel a little underdressed in my black slacks and polo shirt. I don't have any dressy corporate attire because I've only recently left high school, and as I look around at all the people walking the streets of downtown Houston, I realize that clothing is yet another thing I'll have to figure out as I find my dream career. You can't wear yoga pants to work in a skyscraper.

When I was in high school, all I wanted was to grow up and graduate and be an adult, but now I'm realizing that there's so many parts to adulthood that I find stupid. Like corporate clothing.

Of course, the idea of growing old with Liam is a part of being an adult that I can definitely get behind.

"Did your dad design this building?" I ask as we walk up to the elaborate glass entrance of one of Houston's skyscrapers.

"Yep," Liam says, letting me go first into the automatic doors.

The lobby is made of white marble and glass, with water fountains and planted palm trees. The whole building is a little bit excessive, but I guess it's pretty to look at. Liam has made an appointment for us with a woman named Lara Radford, and we sign in at the front desk and then take the elevators up to the sixteenth floor.

Lara is a middle-aged woman with short brown hair, bronzed skin, and bright red lipstick. Everything about her is perfectly put together, from her designer pants suit to her hair and makeup. She's absolutely stunning.

"It's so nice to meet you," she says, shaking my hand. "Let's go in my office."

Her office is twice the size of my bedroom, and it's fancier than any room in my house. She has a window wall that overlooks Houston, and a massive imposing wooden desk with leather chairs. Her diplomas hang on the wall, and I see she has a bachelor and master's degree in accounting.

Lara tells me all about her job, which is comprised of handling all the finances for Mosely International. It sounds absolutely terrifying. She's dealing with a multimillion-dollar business and all the financial work rests on her shoulders. But you can tell she loves her job with the way her eyes light up when she talks about it. This is a highly educated woman with some massive skills.

Skills I know I don't have.

After about an hour, our meeting is over because she's a busy woman with multiple appointments on her schedule today. I thank her for talking with me and I try to act all enthusiastic until we're back in the elevator.

"What'd you think?" Liam says.

"No. Way."

He laughs. "Yeah, her job sounded intense."

"Not only do I not want to spend that many years in college, there is no way I could handle a company's entire financial portfolio," I say, using the terminology I just learned from my meeting. "That's terrifying."

"For sure," he says, reaching for my hand. "Oh well. We can strike accountant off the list."

I frown. "I'm starting to think I'll never find a job I want."

"Nah, we'll find something."

The elevator doors open and Liam and I are now

facing a dozen men in business suits. They have briefcases and stern looks on their faces and everything. Ew. There's no way I could work in a place like this. I appreciate that these jobs are meant for some people, but I am not one of those people.

Back in the warm spring sunshine, Liam and I walk hand in hand down the streets of downtown Houston. Our state's biggest city isn't as glamourous as NYC, but it's still pretty cool being down here. I wonder if Liam misses his old home in the high-rise condo he used to share with his dad. I don't ask, because I'm not sure I want to hear the answer. He seems happy in Roca Springs with me and his mom's side of the family. I don't want to rock the boat by making him question that.

We follow our noses to the smell of food. There's some kind of popup food truck festival just a few blocks over, and Liam looks at me with his eyes wide. "You hungry?"

"Always," I say, grinning back at him.

We check out the lineup of food offerings and settle on a place that only sells baked potatoes. They have every possible potato you could imagine, from the ultimate bacon lovers, to the pizza lovers, to even a chicken alfredo potato. Liam and I each order something over the top because, why not, and then we find a picnic table at a nearby park to eat.

This little park is only the size of one city block,

but it's well taken care of. Greenery stretches from one side to the other, and the air smells like freshly mown grass, even though all around us are the sights of massive buildings. There's a playground nearby, and the sounds of children playing almost make you forget you're in the middle of a city where people like Lara are working their butt off while wearing fancy suits.

"If the food industry wasn't so scary, I could see myself running a food truck," I say as I stab my fork into my baked potato.

"Why is the food industry scary?" he asks.

I list off the answers on my fingers. "Food inspectors, hot sweaty food trucks, mean customers, bad reviews online…"

"That sounds like you're describing a bad food truck," he says with a laugh. "Just run a good food truck and you'll have good reviews and good food."

I shake my head. "There are mean people everywhere. It's impossible to have totally perfect reviews. Plus, most people only leave a review when they're mad."

"Strike one for the food truck idea," he says. "That's a shame. If my girl ran a food truck, then I'd always have a place to take free food."

I throw my straw wrapper at him. "Dork."

"Why don't you just buy a bunch of food trucks and let other people run them, and then you can get all the free food you want?"

"How would I make money off that?"

Liam shrugs. "I don't know. I've got free food on the brain."

I laugh and take another bite of my potato. It's pretty amazing, especially with all the extra cheese and butter I ordered. "I do like the idea of having my own business though." I think on it as I eat. "Not having some boss lording over me sounds good. Getting to wear whatever I want and not being stuck in corporate clothes... making up the rules... that could be fun."

"Yeah, it would be," Liam says. "I think I want to be my own boss, too."

"Now I just need to figure out what my business would be... which puts me right back in the same problem," I say, stabbing my fork into my food with more force than necessary. "I can't own a business unless I'm passionate about it and I'm not passionate about anything!"

"I think we can still count this day as a win," Liam says. He reaches over and steals a bite of my food, so I steal a bite of his in return. "We both want to be business owners. We're one step closer to figuring out this lifelong career thing."

I tilt my head and watch him. "I wish I had half of your optimism and positivity," I say longingly.

He grins, and it reaches all the way to his eyes. "You have me, and that's pretty much the same thing."

My heart floods with warmth. He's right, in a way. I have him. I have my little, perfect, happy life in Roca Springs. I may not have all the answers, but I have enough to get by. Maybe I don't need them all. Maybe happiness is all that really matters, in the end.

And with Liam, I'm happier than I've ever been.

16

LIAM

The local motocross shop hasn't changed at all since I first came here. That's a comforting part of small-town living. The big city is constantly changing, evolving, and growing into something different. But Roca Springs is home. It's slower here. More friendly.

Mr. Hernandez brightens when he sees me walk into his shop. He's been a fan of mine since the day he first met me. He didn't let the bad PR from when I was briefly on Team FRZ Frame sully his opinion of me.

"Liam!" he says, waving me over to the register. "It's good to see you back, my boy."

"Thanks. It's good to be back." I'm standing in front of the same register where I first saw Bella. Deja vu hits me hard and makes me a little nostalgic. I didn't know her at all that day, but she'd captured my attention from the first second I saw her. I wasn't even looking for a girlfriend, and yet I ended up meeting my soul mate that day.

"You here for some fuel?" Mr. Hernandez says, breaking me out of my daydreams of Bella.

"Yes, sir," I say, taking out my wallet. Five gallons, please."

He rings me up and then we walk out to the back of the shop where the gas pump is located. I set my gas jug on the ground and he starts filling it up.

"Are the rumors true about you moving back here for good?" he asks.

"Yep. I'm out of the professional motocross scene. It just wasn't my thing. I like being here with my family more."

He's a cool guy, and not some gossip monger, so I don't mind telling him the details of my life. He nods eagerly and gives me a smile that reminds me of my late grandfather. That man always seemed proud of me no matter what I did.

"You made a good call, son. The fame is fun, but family is more important."

"Now I just need a job."

"What kind of job?" he says, screwing the lid back on my gas jug. "We're hiring here, but it's only part time."

"Seriously? Part time would be perfect while I'm still in college. Could I maybe apply for the job?"

Mr. Hernandez claps his hands together in front

of his chest. "You kiddin' me? I'd hire you in a heart-beat. I don't need an application. When can you start?"

I laugh. "I can start work after tomorrow's race."

He claps me on the back as we walk back toward the front of the shop. "Perfect. I'm happy to have you, boy. I'll get three times the business with you working here."

"And here I thought you were being nice," I say with a laugh.

He walks with me back to my truck, which is parked just a few feet away. "My daughter makes the schedule. Just get with her tomorrow and pick your own hours. She'll show you the ropes around here."

"Sounds good. Thank you." I reach out and shake his hand.

"What are you going to college for?" he asks.

I shrug. "I'm not sure yet. I'd love to work in motocross, but if I'm not a pro racer, I'm not sure what I'd do."

"Now that you mention it..." Mr. Hernandez rubs his chin as he studies me. "I heard a rumor that the owner of Oakcreek Motocross Park is looking to sell it soon."

"Yeah... I heard that, too."

"You should buy it. We need a guy like you running the track. You could breathe new life into it."

"You think so?" I ask, feeling the idea invigorate

my soul. Having just been at Oakcreek last weekend, I haven't been able to stop thinking about it. That track is awesome. The terrain is beautiful and the track is well designed. It's a lot more popular than our local Roca Springs track.

"You'd be perfect for the job," he says. "Plus, you could hire me to provide all your race fuel! We could all partner up. Even get Roca Springs MX in on it. We could make a series race or something, and everyone can come to my shop to get their fuel and bike parts!"

"That would be fun," I say with a nod. "Maybe I'll reach out to him soon. Do you know his name?"

"I'll do you even better," he says, taking his phone out of his shirt pocket. "I've got his number. You give him a call and tell him Jim Hernandez referred you."

IT TAKES ME THREE DAYS TO GET THE COURAGE TO call the owner of Oakcreek Motocross Park. I don't know why I'm so scared about it. I guess I'm afraid no one in their right mind would sell a teenager their well-established motocross track. Of course, if I can work out a deal to buy it after I graduate, then I won't be a teenager. I'll be a slightly older college graduate.

I'm not kidding myself on the costs involved. I'm sure it'll be a lot of money to buy a business that big, but I still have most of my Team Loco money saved, and now I'm working at the shop part time, so I'll save up even more money. Whatever it takes, I'll find a way to get the down payment.

I haven't told Bella yet, either. I'm afraid of what she might say, and I want to have all my ducks in a row before I tell her about this crazy idea of mine. So the next day after work, before I drive over to her place to take her and my little brothers to see a movie, I close and lock my bedroom door and then I take a deep breath and call John Avery, the owner of Oakcreek.

When he answers, I introduce myself.

"Ah, Liam Mosely," he says with a chuckle. He has a deep, raspy voice. "I've been expecting your call."

"Really?"

"Yes, sir. Jim Hernandez hasn't shut up about you. Apparently, he's been telling you to buy my track."

Well, I guess that's one way to break the ice. "He did mention it," I say, trying to sound confident on the phone. Ever since I started thinking about owning my own motocross track, it's all I've been thinking about. I can't imagine a better career. Working for myself, in the sport I love. I'd get to ride my bike every day, and still make money from it. And sure, I could always get some land and make my own track from scratch, but buying an established track with name recognition would be much easier.

"Are you interested in selling the track in a few years?"

"It'll be a hard thing to let go, but unfortunately I'll have to sell it soon. I'm getting too old. I can't keep up with it like I used to. My wife says I should retire already so we can travel and all that crap she wants to do."

"I'd love to talk with you about buying it," I say. "I still have a few years of college left, but after that—"

"I'd be happy to sell it to you, son," he says before I can finish my well-rehearsed thoughts.

"Really?"

"I don't have any kids to leave it to. I don't want to just sell to some investor. This place is my heart and soul, kid. I want it to go to someone who loves motocross as much as I do. Someone who will run my track with love and care and keep the sport alive. Can you do that?"

"Yes, sir. I know I can."

"Then consider it yours. I'll give you a real cheap price, too."

I thank him several times, and the rest of our conversation just flies by. He tells me about the financials and the logistics of running a track. He says his wife does all the office stuff, and he has a few part time employees who will probably stay on when I buy the place. The idea is even more exciting when he tells me about what his wife does. She maintains the website, keeps up with the paperwork, and basically runs the track from a business stand-point while he works the tractor and maintains the property.

Bella wanted to work a job where she could be the boss but get to do her own thing. Working the track with me would be exactly that kind of job. We could do this together. We could own it together. This could be the opportunity that both of us have been looking for.

17

BELLA

"*B*ella."

Liam's whisper is soft and far away. I hear it again. Then my body gently shakes. My eyes flutter open and I hear Liam's voice for real, right next to me. "Bella, wake up."

It wasn't a dream.

I roll over in bed and see my boyfriend standing here, in my bedroom, at—I look at the time on my phone—seven in the morning?

"What is wrong with you?" I say rolling back over and burying my head in my pillow. "It's so early."

He sits on the edge of my bed. "Wake up, babe. I have one final career adventure for you."

I roll back over and glare at him. What can I say? I'm not a morning person. "How did you even get inside my house this early?"

He smirks. "Your brother let me in."

I roll my eyes and tug the blankets up to my face. "I liked it better when he hated you," I mumble.

Liam laughs and then leans over and kisses my forehead. "Rise and shine, my love. This is going to be an amazing day. I have found the career to end all careers. You're going to love it."

With a yawn, I sit up and watch him standing there all eager and basically spilling over with excitement. It's way too early in the morning for this kind of joy.

"What kind of career?" I ask skeptically.

He shakes his head. "I can't tell you. It's a surprise. I have to show you."

I yawn again. "Do I have to dress nice?"

He shakes his head. "That's just one of the many benefits of this career. You can wear whatever you want."

"Well...that's enough to convince me," I say, throwing off the covers. I am immensely grateful that I wore decent pajamas to bed last night, otherwise Liam could have seen me looking really stupid with a baggy Mickey Mouse shirt or something otherwise horrible.

"Get dressed," Liam says, opening my bedroom door. "I'll be waiting out here. There's coffee and donuts in my truck."

My curiosity is on high alert as I tug on some

jeans and a shirt. The rest of these little career adventures have mostly been for fun, but Liam is acting like this one is a big deal. What had he called it? A career to end all careers? How can he make that kind of statement when he knows how impossibly impossible it has been finding a job I like?

But I want to trust him, so I brush my teeth and throw on some makeup and then meet him in the living room. He's sitting with my brother, who is showing him his one-legged squats.

Now that Brent gets to start physical therapy on his foot in a few weeks, he's been preparing by doing squats with his good leg and lifting barbells and working out the rest of his body from the couch. My brother has always been an early bird, hitting the gym before school. He's weird like that. My mom and I do not share that trait and we prefer to sleep in as late as possible.

"Ya'll have fun," Brent says, waving to us as we leave. I'm still not used to this nice version of my brother who likes my boyfriend. But it's nice.

Liam's truck smells like sugary, coffee goodness, and we snack on donuts while we drive out of town, heading west. I'm trying to pick up on clues as to where we're going, but there's an entire half of the country in this direction. It could be anything.

"Is it scuba diving?" I ask.

"There's not an ocean in this direction."

I bite my lip. "Is it puppy training? I could totally be a puppy trainer."

"No, but that is a cool idea."

"Is it the circus?" I ask after our trip reaches its first hour of being on the road. I've asked about a hundred questions so far, and none of them have been correct.

He snorts. "No, but it's a fun thought. I know exactly which sideshow circus attraction you'd be the star of."

I cross my arms over my chest. "And what would that be?"

"Hear ye, hear ye," Liam calls out like he's some kind of PT Barnum circus guy. "Gather around and see our newest, most annoying attraction. It's Bella Castro – the girl who has zero patience for surprises! Her sheer lack of patience will astound you!"

I burst out laughing. "You're a nerd."

"I'm your nerd," he says, winking at me.

He takes the next exit, which is vaguely familiar. As soon as we turn off the main road and take a left, we're in the middle of the hill country. Chills prickle over my arms. "We're close to Oakcreek Motocross Park," I say.

His eyebrows lift while he's watching the road. "Yep."

"There's not much else out here," I say, looking out the window. "This town is a lot like Roca

Springs… just all country town and fields of open land."

"Yep," he says again, not looking at me.

"What kind of career is out here?" I ask.

He tisks. "You and your impatience…"

"Sorry," I say, leaning my head against his shoulder. "I'll shut up."

Liam turns into the driveway that leads into the motocross park. "We're here."

I stare at him for a moment, waiting for him to laugh and say he's just kidding. There's not really a career at a motocross track. I'm not going to become a pro racer or anything. He didn't even like that career for himself. So why are we here?

"I don't get it."

Liam parks his truck next to the main office building which is where you pay to ride or sign up for a race. But we don't have our bikes with us today, so we can't ride. He turns to face me, and when our eyes meet, I can tell he's nervous. It's written all over his face, and swimming around in his eyes. He's nervous of whatever he's about to tell me.

"What is it?" I say, reaching for his hand. They're warm and a little sweaty. Wow. "Liam?"

He clears his throat. "Okay so… I think I found the perfect career for me and you. But… only if you're on board."

"I'm listening."

He takes a deep breath. "I want to buy this track."

My eyes widen. "Okay…"

"I want to buy it and run it. Not now, but in a few years when I'm done with college. I want you to run it with me. We'd have to move out here and it'd be a full-time job, but it would be so fun. I've been talking with the owner and his wife does half the work and you'd get to be your own boss and we could just apprentice with them until we figure it out and— "

"Babe," I say, cutting him off.

His brows are flattened with apprehension. I squeeze his hands. "You don't have to convince me," I say. "I am totally on board."

His lips stretch into a grin. "Really?"

I nod excitedly. "Oh my God, totally. One hundred percent. Are you kidding me? We could run our own track!"

"I know!" He bites his bottom lip and we sit here and smile at each other, both overflowing with excitement. "It would be amazing," he says.

"It would be so amazing. We could be our own bosses… Liam it's perfect. You were right. This is my perfect career."

"And you'd be fine moving out here with me?" he asks, swallowing. "In a couple years, of course."

"Yes," I say. "It's not too far from our families. Let's do it."

"And then one day we could… well you know," he says with a little awkward shrug. "We could maybe get married and run it together like the owners do now. In the future of course. When you're ready."

I make this goofy grin and put a hand to my chest. "Liam! Are you saying you might propose to me one day?"

"Yes," he says quickly. "I am definitely, definitely saying that. I don't care if we've only been together a few months and if it's too soon for that and if I haven't even..." He stops himself with a shake of his head. "Look, I know it's early, but you're my girl. You're my heart. My everything. I want to make these plans with you. And I hope that doesn't scare you away."

"I'm not scared at all," I say. I slide across the truck seat and crawl into his lap. "In fact…" I take a breath. "I love you, Liam Mosely."

His eyes widen and then he shakes his head. "No… no… I was supposed to say that first. I've been waiting for the right moment…"

I lace my fingers behind his head and smile at him. "You waited too long, my dear. I beat you to it."

He sighs. "I love you, Bella. I should have said it first but I totally do."

I grin. "Hey, this is an equal opportunity relationship. I get to be romantic, too."

His arms tighten around me as he presses his forehead to mine. "I guess we're now officially in a competition to see who can be the most romantic."

I grin. "That sounds fun."

"Everything with you is fun."

I press my lips to his. "I love you," I say again, just because I can.

His chestnut brown eyes sparkle as he looks right into my soul. "I love you, too."

Three Months Later

LIAM

IT'S THE PERFECT SUMMER DAY FOR AN OUTDOOR picnic. Mom was more than happy to host today's lunch since Phil just finished building her a long picnic table that fits perfectly in the middle of her garden. The weather has been perfect for gardening, and Mom's flowers are in full bloom.

She's showing off some purple flowers to Bella's mom, and they're both talking about how beautiful they are. It's pretty awesome how our families are getting along so well. My mom invited Bella's mom to join a local book club a couple months ago, and they've been inseparable ever since.

I slide my metal spatula under the burgers to check to see if it's time to flip them. Phil has a state-of-the-art grill and every time I cook on it, I tell myself that I'll buy one just like it for when Bella and I move out to Oakcreek in a couple of years.

"Go long," Brent calls out as he prepares to throw the football at my little brother. "Go longer than that, kid."

Dylan runs further into the backyard, then braces himself to catch the ball. Brent has found a good friend in my little brother. They both love football I addition to motocross. Matt likes dirt bikes more though, so he's been teaming up with me to convince our parents to let him get his own dirt bike. Little does he know, my mom told me they're getting him one for his seventh birthday in a few months. The little kid is going to be so psyched. I'll take him under my wing and teach him everything I know, but I won't pressure him into thinking he has to make a career out of it.

Bella walks out of my backdoor, holding a bright pink pitcher and a stack of matching pink plastic cups. "The sweet tea is ready! And it's extra sweet, which is the way all tea should be, if you ask me."

"Woohoo," My mom says. She takes the pitcher from her and pours herself a glass. "Thanks, sweetheart."

"No problem."

Bella flashes me a smile and walks over. She's wearing a pale yellow sundress that shows off her golden tan. The local track offered another discount season pass for the summer and we've been taking advantage of the deal and going to ride almost every day. At night, we cuddle, watch Netflix, and talk about our plans for our future track.

My old teammate Jett even put us in contact with his parents who own their own motocross track on the other side of the state. They're going to teach us what they know about running a successful motocross business, and maybe one day in the future, we can all host a series race together.

"The food smells good," Bella says, sliding her arm around me. "And you look extremely handsome. The apron is telling the truth."

I laugh and look down at myself. I'm wearing Phil's oversized grilling apron that says, "World's most handsome cook." It was a novelty gift my mom gave him last Christmas. Perched on my head is a pair of cheap lime green sunglasses that Matt asked me to hold onto for him while he went to play in the water sprinkler. I take them off and slide them over my eyes.

"You think this look is sexy?" I say.

"Nope," she says, holding back a laugh. "But the apron says you're handsome, so I guess I have to believe it."

I laugh and put the sunglasses on top of her head. She kisses me on the cheek and then opens a package of paper plates and starts handing them out to everyone. "Food is ready!" she calls out to her brother and Dylan, who are still throwing the football.

I stack up the burgers on a plate and carry them to the picnic table that Bella has arranged all neatly. There's burger buns, lettuce, cheese, pickles, and condiments all laid out next to several bags of chips.

My family and her mom and brother all gather around and we sit down together and eat. There's laughter and jokes and a few embarrassing stories of my childhood that my mom just can't help but share with everyone. I look over at Bella, and she smiles up at me. It's funny how life happens.

One day you're training hard for a goal you've wanted your entire life, and then the next day you're throwing that goal away, in favor of something else. Something simple. Backyard picnics and little brothers and the one girl you met on accident one day and fell so hard for that you knew you couldn't live without her.

Life doesn't always turn out the way you planned it.

No. Sometimes, it turns out better.

Amy Sparling is the bestselling author of books for teens and the teens at heart. She lives on the coast of Texas with her family, her spoiled rotten pets, and a huge pile of books. She graduated with a degree in English and has worked at a bookstore, coffee shop, and a fashion boutique. Her fashion skills aren't the best, but luckily she turned her love of coffee and books into a writing career that means she can work in her pajamas. Her favorite things are coffee, book boyfriends, and Netflix binges.

She's always loved reading books from R. L. Stine's Fear Street series, to The Baby Sitter's Club series by Ann, Martin, and of course, Twilight. She started writing her own books in 2010 and now publishes several books a year. Amy loves getting messages from her readers and responds to every single one! Connect with her on one of the links below.